Torch Job

Patricia Rosemoor

Harlequin Books

TORONTO • NEW YORK • LONDON
AMSTERDAM • PARIS • SYDNEY • HAMBURG
STOCKHOLM • ATHENS • TOKYO • MILAN
MADRID • WARSAW • BUDAPEST • AUCKLAND

To the artists who lost their life's work in the fire
that leveled the River North gallery building.
I'll never forget the column of smoke visible from
miles away... nor will I forget the
devastation afterward.

Harlequin Intrigue edition published March 1993

ISBN 0-373-22219-X

TORCH JOB

Printed in U.S.A.

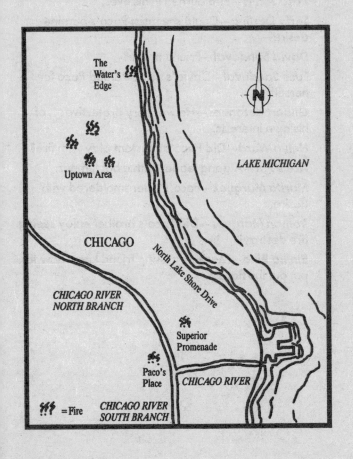

The Water's Edge

Uptown Area

LAKE MICHIGAN

CHICAGO

CHICAGO RIVER
NORTH BRANCH

North Lake Shore Drive

Superior
Promenade

Paco's
Place

CHICAGO RIVER

🔥🔥 = Fire   CHICAGO RIVER
SOUTH BRANCH

N

CAST OF CHARACTERS

Paco Jones—Fire burned in his eyes.

Taffy Darling—Could she resist Paco's burning desire?

David Sandoval—Friend or foe?

Luce Sandoval—David's sister wanted Paco for herself.

Gilbert Koroneos—He was very protective . . . of his own interests.

Helen Ward—Did Paco's assistant play with fire?

Ace Vigil—A gang leader with a hot temper.

Marita Marquez—Paco's sister smoldered with desire.

Ramon Marquez—Did Paco's brother enjoy seeing fire destroy?

Emilia Pino—Marita's missing friend knew how to put out the flames.

Chapter One

Nine-thirty-five. Near-deserted streets. The rumble of an elevated train overhead shattering the quiet…then silence once more.

Satisfied that all was going according to schedule, he stubbed out his cigarette and started the car. With a last cautious look around, he pulled the vehicle behind the former warehouse and parked in the shadows of the loading dock and trash bins. The muted orange glow from streetlights at either end of the alley lit up the road and assured him there were no unwanted witnesses around. He opened the trunk and unloaded his simple tools—three gallons of paint remover, a box of large resealable plastic baggies and a roll of waxed paper.

Anticipation sluiced through him. His heart was hammering, his blood pumping. The buzz was mounting. A deep breath settled him down temporarily. Breaking into the empty building would be a piece of cake. He was in control. In his element. He worked swiftly and with the precision of experience, mentally ticking off each completed objective.

Alarms detached. Door released. Him inside.

The building was dark but for the faint glow coming from the hallway. Using a flashlight, he slipped into the basement and shut down the sprinkler system. Back on the first floor, he doused his beam and followed the emergency lights to the front of the building, to the atrium that was the focal point of Superior Promenade. The area was subtly washed by moonlight pouring in through the plate glass walls—enough so he could see locked galleries lining the large open space with its flagstone floor and metal waterfall sculpture.

The liquid trickle of the fountain echoed up through all four stories.

He didn't want any water to interfere with his plans, so he located the valve to shut off the fountain. Stuck. Putting his weight into the effort, he budged the valve but knocked his shoulder into the sculpture. A loose piece went flying and smacked into the wall. The crash followed by a lighter metallic clanking reverberated up the atrium.

He froze. And took a deep breath. The building was empty.

Sweating anyway, he picked the locks of the half-dozen galleries that had been chosen in advance. He was as nervous as he was psyched. Unrolling the waxed paper, he laid trailers from each room back to the atrium. Carefully he poured paint remover into the plastic bags and resealed them. Placing several in each gallery at the end of the waxed paper spokes, he pricked the baggies with a pin. Paint remover dribbled drop by drop onto the homemade fuses.

Back in the atrium away from the fumes, cans gathered for a quick escape, he prepared himself for an experience that would be almost spiritual. Certainly physical. His hand shook slightly as it dived deep into his trouser pocket.

Pulling out the lighter, he torched the first trailer of waxed paper.

"URSULA, you *are* going to make our fall gala Friday night, aren't you?" Taffy Darling wheedled into the telephone receiver. "It's my first event for Superior Promenade." Anxious that the opening for the sixteen art galleries housed in Superior Promenade be a success, she was dismayed by a crash from another part of the building. Obviously someone else was working late on a display. Getting her mind back on target, she added, "The festivities won't be the same without you."

"Are you trying to enlist my sympathies?" the Chicago talk show host asked.

"So what if I am? Didn't I give you a great idea for that show about 'Poor Little Rich Girls'?"

Ursula laughed. "As I recall, you enjoyed your moment of glory on camera. And didn't that show help you get your new job?"

"You mean my *only* job ever." Reminded of the loss of her trust fund, Taffy sighed. "Come on, Ursula, be a friend. At twenty-eight I don't have time to build a career. I'm just jumping in blindly and praying I land on both feet."

"That's what I like about you. You never give up. All right, you can count on us. We'll be there."

"Oh, thank you! You're such a love."

Dropping the receiver into its cradle, Taffy took a relieved breath that turned into a yawn. So many

things to do, so little time. Two days to be exact. The
invitations and press releases were out, but she had
more follow-up work. Now she could call her other
media contacts and truthfully tell them Ursula Black
would be there. The talk show host's presence would
get Taffy the publicity she needed.

But as coordinator of special events for Superior
Promenade, she still had to make last-minute checks
on the decorations, the caterers and the entertain-
ment. Coordinator. What a joke. As if she had a staff.
Truth was, she was the entire special events department, had talked her way into a position that hadn't
before existed. Having wealthy and even famous contacts had been enough to convince the multi-gallery
building management to give her idea a try.

Now she just had to prove herself!

Taffy yawned again and her eyes watered. Sheer
exhaustion was setting in, a product of long hours and
late nights at the job. She would close her eyes for a
tiny moment. Then she would take care of those phone
calls. But even as her head drifted lower and was cradled by her arms resting on her desk, even as she half
dozed, hazy thoughts whirled through her tired mind.
She had to check on that extra security. And had she
made a mistake not auditioning the musicians and the
tarot-card reader personally?

Finally letting go, Taffy floated off, her last thought
anxious: she had less than forty-eight hours to get
every little detail together or her newly created job
would go right up in smoke....

OLD AND FILLED with flammable contents, Superior
Promenade would burn fast. He was burning with ex-

hilaration as he escaped back out to the alley. But his excitement stilled as he reached into his pocket for the car keys and found nothing. He dropped the containers to free both hands to search. No key ring.

He mentally retraced his steps inside the building. He remembered the shutoff valve . . . and the crash followed by a metallic clanking that now held a new significance. The key ring must have escaped his jacket when he rammed his shoulder into the sculpture. It had to be somewhere on the atrium floor.

Knowing that it was only a matter of moments before someone noticed the smoke, he was tempted to run, to leave the car behind in hopes that the fire would engulf it, too. No guarantees, though. And, while the car didn't belong to him anyway, he might have left something identifying inside. Fingerprints, certainly. He had to get the car out of there. Had to get his keys.

He had to go back inside the burning building . . . a challenge he'd never faced before!

The concept filled him with a peculiar thrill, and renewed inner heat consumed him as he raced against time.

Smoke.

The tiny moment of repose stretched until the distinct odor of smoke teased Taffy awake. She was muzzy and disoriented as she lifted her head from the desk and focused on her surroundings. Everything seemed normal. Maybe she had been dreaming. Then she sniffed the air. The permeating scent was real. A fire nearby. But where? Certainly not in the building. No alarms pierced the silence.

Still trying to focus, she rose from her desk, crossed the expanse of the second-floor office and threw open the door.

"God!"

A thick gray curtain rose up toward the fourth-floor skylights. She shot to the rail and looked down into the flames that crackled and danced in a ring around the atrium. The very walls appeared to be alive. Smoke filled her lungs. Made her throat spasm and her eyes burn. She had to get out!

Panic waited a pulse beat away as she went for the stairs, clogged with smoke but still free of fire. Trying not to cough, not even to breathe, she took them two at a time until she had to release her hold on the metal railing when its warmth became unbearable heat. Chest squeezed by an invisible fist, she descended toward the inferno, her gaze wildly skipping from gallery window to gallery window through which she could see pieces of artwork being consumed like tasty appetizers.

The fire seemed to be a living, breathing entity. The low, pulsating roar surrounding her made Taffy think she had descended into the belly of some beast.

Escape. She had to escape. But which way out? Front or back? Did it even matter? Flames shot out at her from every direction and she felt trapped in their midst. A gallery window exploded, covering her with shattered glass. Though she could barely see her way, she knew the front door was closer. Covering her nose and mouth with her scarf, narrowing her eyes into protective slits, she ducked her head and made a run for it.

An obstacle brought her to a crashing halt. The fountain. Trying to steady herself, she grabbed at the sculpture, then snatched her hands away from the even hotter metal.

Running footsteps behind her competed with the roar of the fire. She turned to spy a dark figure coming toward her. Savior or arsonist? She didn't know. He stopped and bent over, as if retrieving something, then straightened, a large object in his gloved hand. He advanced on her.

Instinct pushed her forward toward the front door. She was almost there—within arm's reach—when a blow to her neck brought her to her knees. Gasping in pain, she tried to stand. He was closer now, looming over her. She barely got a glimpse of him before a second blow, this on the back of her head, made the tile floor rush up to meet her.

"THEN IT'S SETTLED?" Paco Jones glanced at his watch. Quarter to ten. They'd been in the coffee shop for nearly an hour and he was anxious to get a move on.

"As far as I'm concerned, you can set a date for that fund-raiser any time you want," Bill Long told Luce Sandoval. "I'll be happy to provide the space."

Bill owned Endeavors, the gallery where Paco's personal photographs were on display. And Luce was an old friend. A recently elected Chicago alderwoman, she was trying to raise the money necessary to properly address the gang issue in her mid-north neighborhood. Paco had readily agreed to arrange the meeting between Luce and Bill because he believed in what she was trying to do. He suspected she hoped he had other, more personal reasons in mind.

She turned her sharp hazel gaze on him, gave him a smile that was most definitely personal. "What do you think, Paco? How soon should we plan for the fund-raiser?"

"That's up to you. I'll do what I can, but it's your baby."

Luce quickly masked her disappointment, and Paco wondered why he wasn't attracted to her in the way she so obviously wanted him to be. She'd changed from a manipulative teenager who thought the world owed her the good life to a woman who solicited responsibility. She'd always been easy on the eyes, her pastel outfits contrasting with the dark exoticism she'd inherited from her Hispanic and Native American ancestors.

So what was wrong with his healthy male libido that he wasn't tempted to taste what she had so subtly yet surely offered more than once in recent months? Maybe he couldn't get past the fact that she was David's kid sister.

Maybe he was just plain loco.

"Why don't I get back to you?" she suggested to Bill. "I'd like to go over the details with my press assistant, Gilbert Koroneos. I'm certain he'll have some concrete ideas to contribute."

Paco's jaw tightened at the mention of Koroneos. He didn't like the man. Too slick and cool.

"That'll be just fine, Alderwoman Sandoval," Bill said.

"Please, you must call me Luce."

"All right." The middle-aged man was entranced, if his expression were any indication. "Luce."

Bill rose and held Luce's chair while Paco got the check and took it to the register. He figured he ought to offer Luce a ride home rather than let her take a taxi, but as he joined the gallery owner and alderwoman on the street, a car pulled up to the curb. The electric passenger window whined its way down and the driver leaned across the front seat.

"Hey, Paco, how's it going?" David Sandoval asked a little too brightly, as if he were forcing himself to be sociable.

"Not bad," Paco said. "Luce has a location for her fund-raiser."

"This is Bill Long, the very generous owner of Endeavors," Luce said, her voice a bit odd. "Bill, my brother, David."

"Nice to meet you," Bill said, bending over.

"Same here."

But Paco thought the smile David flashed was as unnatural as his forced cheer.

Back in high school, the two of them had been inseparable. They were still friends, though they saw each other less and less frequently due to their diverse interests. David was a social worker and still lived in and was involved with the community where they all grew up, while Paco worked as a commercial photographer, his business and living quarters based in a neighborhood west of the Loop. Even so, Paco always felt the old camaraderie surface when he and David got together.

Tonight, however, was different.

Luce didn't pretend she was glad to see her brother. "What are you doing here, David?" she asked, her words clipped.

"I knew you'd need a ride, Lucky."

"Luce," she hissed, clearly irritated by his using her old high school nickname. "I'm capable of taking care of myself. I would have gotten home safely."

"I was going to volunteer to drive her home," Bill said, seemingly oblivious to the fact that David appeared strained and Luce angry.

Paco wondered what was going on between those two. A sibling conflict of some sort? He wasn't about to stick around and find out. The Sandovals had always had volatile tempers when they crossed each other, and Paco would rather not be around when they erupted. He opened the passenger door of David's car and indicated Luce should get in.

"I'm glad things worked out the way you wanted them," he told her.

"Well...almost." She stepped down off the curb but stalled getting into her brother's car. "Paco, there's a charity ball next week. It's for a cause dear to my heart, to raise money for shelters for battered women and their children." She opened her purse and reached inside. "I'd like to give you a ticket, if you'll agree to come."

"Sure. I'll *buy* two tickets," he said deliberately so that she wouldn't get the wrong idea. He was certain she'd have no trouble finding another escort, just as he'd have no trouble finding a date.

Luce didn't meet his eyes immediately, and he sensed her frustration. But when she pulled her hand from the purse, it held a pair of tickets, and her features were composed, her lips softly curved into a smile.

"Here you go."

Paco took the tickets and slipped them inside his lightweight leather bomber jacket. "I can send you a check?"

"Of course. If I couldn't trust *you*..."

She shrugged and slid into the front seat. David said something low in Spanish, but Paco didn't catch the words, only the tone that made him uncomfortable. He closed the door and waved them off with a sense of relief as David gunned the accelerator and the vehicle shot off into the night.

"I envy you," Bill said as they crossed the street and headed for the next block where Endeavors was located in Superior Promenade. "That's a woman any man would be nuts to pass up if he had a shot at her."

Because he didn't want to analyze why he'd done exactly that, Paco made a joke of the situation. "You know us artists. We're all crazy."

"You're a particularly talented crazy man, but then I guess you know that. When the press gets a load of your work Friday night, everyone in the city who counts will be aware of it, too."

"Trying to turn my head, Bill?"

"Just trying to be truthful. Not many photographers have your insight."

Paco hoped Bill was correct both about his talent and about the press he would get from his first major exhibition. While he made a good living from advertising photography, his personal satisfaction came from using his camera to capture statements about poverty and its social impact on people.

Having grown up in, and having freed himself from, the stranglehold of the ghetto, Paco was determined to make mainstream Chicagoans sit up and take notice of what went on in the dark, dangerous pockets in every corner of their city.

Paco didn't fool himself into thinking he could change the world. At least not overnight. He only hoped that somehow, someday, he would make a difference to someone. He would go to any risk to get a photograph he thought important. He had already put himself in dangerous situations more than once, and he would do so again if necessary.

"Hey, is that smoke?" Bill suddenly asked, his worried voice breaking into Paco's thoughts.

"Where?"

"The gallery building!"

Paco's eyes widened. He saw it, too. Both men ran across the street, which was free of other bystanders.

"Maybe it's not a big fire," Bill muttered as he ran. "Maybe the sprinkler system will put it out."

But the black flume of smoke escaping the building was ominous. "I don't think so," Paco muttered, putting on some speed. "And it doesn't look like anyone's called the fire department."

"Paco, wait a minute!"

Paco didn't know why he was so anxious to get closer. He didn't even have his camera. The displays inside—maybe it wasn't too late to salvage some of them. Artists would lose their life's work. At least he had the negatives to his photographs. They would have nothing.

"Paco, you crazy?" Bill puffed, now a ways behind him. "This might be a serious fire. Let's cross the street before it's too late."

"You go. Find a telephone!" Paco yelled. "Call 911."

Some gut-deep instinct that had nothing to do with the building's contents drove him toward the main entrance. Heat already radiated from the building, though the blaze wasn't visible until he was practically at the plate glass wall of the atrium. Then he could see the flames dancing their way up toward the fourth-floor skylights, the red glow flickering through the column of thick black smoke.

He was mere steps away from the door and slowing before realizing how ludicrous his actions were. He could get himself killed. Besides, Bill was the one with the keys and the front doors would, of course, be locked. He might as well get to safety.

But, as he turned away from the entrance, something bright and out of place caught his attention.

Moving closer, he squinted to make out the oddity through the living gray-black curtain. Pale strands that looked like blond hair spilled across the floor. He pressed up against the hot glass and was able to make out the shape of a woman, facedown, not far from the door. The fire had not yet reached her. Fingers of flame crawled ever closer as they devoured a nearby fallen beam.

Not stopping to consider whether or not she might even be alive, Paco went for the door. The metal handle seared his fingers and he gave up that approach. Instead he rammed the door with his shoulder...to no avail. The lock wouldn't budge. Any harder and the glass itself might split . . . not to mention what it could do to him. He backed off and scoured the street for Bill, but the gallery owner had disappeared, hopefully at a telephone. Paco realized that he, alone, would be responsible for whatever happened to that woman.

Trying to stay calm and focused, Paco looked for some tool dense enough to penetrate plate glass. There were no convenient bricks or boards lying around. Then he spotted what he needed. A parking-meter thief had been scavenging this side of the street—several meter tops had been removed totally—but must have been interrupted while still at work. One meter head sat crookedly on its base.

Paco grabbed the heavy metal part and easily tore it free from its mooring. Then, using all his strength, he pitched it at the building. The window shattered, the glass surrounding the modest hole spiderwebbing in an ever-spreading circle. Slowly the cracked glass began to sink from its own weight. Pieces tinkled like the notes of a macabre wind chime as they hit the cement sidewalk. The opening was still not big enough to chance without danger of severing a limb.

Whipping off his bomber jacket, Paco used the garment as a shield. The tough leather protected both his head and the fists that pounded at the cracked glass, widening the hole until it was large enough to effect a rescue.

Even as he hesitated on the sidewalk, heat blasted him. Wasting no time, taking one last deep breath of outside air, he stepped into the raging inferno and went for the woman's body. Covered with soot, she lay still as death. The tongues of fire surrounding her keened as if in mourning.

Paco didn't bother to check for vital signs, merely covered the woman's head and torso with the protective leather, then lifted the slight figure and anchored his bundle against his chest. Hunching into her, feeling as if he were being set on fire himself, he left the way he'd come.

Once free of the inferno, Paco ran for the other side of the street, wheezing and coughing all the way.

"Good God!" Bill shouted as he ran toward Paco. "Someone was inside?"

Paco gasped in the fresh air. "She was lying near the door as if she were trying to get out."

And from the fresh blood smearing his sleeve as he gently set her down on the sidewalk, Paco figured someone had deliberately prevented her from achieving that objective. He placed his face next to her mouth, hoping to feel her breath against his cheek.

"Is she alive?" Bill asked anxiously.

"She's not breathing."

"Can't you do something? The fire department will be here any minute."

Sirens were already wailing in the distance as Paco tilted her head back to open her airway, pinched her nose and covered her mouth with his own. She smelled like burning wood, tasted like charcoal. A few more moments and she would have been kindling. But she wasn't. She was a human being. One he'd rescued. She had to live. He forced his own oxygen deep down into her lungs.

"Come on, breathe!" he muttered as he came up for air.

She looked so young, so delicate, so helpless lying there in his arms, her lush ponytail streaked with soot. He couldn't actually make out the features beneath the grime, but even in her stillness, he got the impression of an impudently tilted nose and a determined chin. He covered her mouth and tried again—and again felt no response.

"I risked my life to get you out of that building, lady! The least you could do is breathe, damn it!"

As if responding to his demand, she coughed in his face. Paco went limp with relief.

"Thank God!"

"You did it!" Bill shouted. "Paco, in addition to being one damned fine artist you're a real-life hero!"

The woman he saved continued to cough as the fire engines pulled up to the building and the melee began. Her eyes fluttered open.

Rather than thanking Paco for saving her hide, the blonde struggled, hoarsely shouting, "Let go of me, you bastard!"

Surprised, Paco loosened his grip only to have a fist land right in the middle of his throat.

Chapter Two

"What was that for?" the man looming over her demanded angrily.

"Don't touch me!" Taffy said, scooting back from him.

An uncontrollable coughing fit took her breath away and left her wheezing. Her head began to throb. Blinking at the stranger who kept his distance, she gradually came to her senses. No longer inside the burning building, she was on the sidewalk opposite Superior Promenade. Several fire engines and trucks and dozens of fire and police personnel swarmed the area. Streams of water from hoses pelted the gallery building from various directions, but the effort appeared useless against the viciousness of the flames.

"Listen, miss, Paco just saved your life." This came from a paunchy middle-aged man who stood to one side. Taffy thought he looked familiar.

"Paco," she echoed, trying out the name.

She took a better look at her supposed savior who knelt before her. Black hair, black eyes. An arrestingly handsome face, his features strong and seemingly carved of granite. An equally impressive body.

Maybe that's why he frightened her, because of his virility.

A sudden vision in which she was surrounded by flames flashed through her mind...receded and stayed just out of reach.

"You saved my life?" she asked with a frown.

But his friend didn't give him the chance to answer. "He pulled you out of that burning building—"

"Then you were inside?" Taffy's eyes locked with Paco's. Fear crawled through her once more. She hadn't been alone. That much she was certain of.

"And he gave you mouth-to-mouth because you'd stopped breathing," the other man finished.

"Tell me," she whispered, confused and anxious, her chest feeling as if a ton of bricks had been dropped on it.

"We were on our way back to Bill's gallery when we saw the fire," Paco finally said. "He went to call the fire department. I stuck around."

"And you came back inside anyway?" It hurt to talk. Her throat was raw. "Why?"

"I saw you sprawled across the floor facedown. You were out cold."

"You risked your life to save mine," she whispered.

"I did what anyone would do."

"I don't believe that." For the first time, Taffy realized how close she had come to death. "I don't know how to thank you."

"You just did."

He rose and held out a hand. She let him help her up to her feet. She was so woozy.

"Sorry about hitting you. I thought..."

Her words trailed off and she frowned as the vision flickered at the back of her mind once more. And once more the lights went out and she was left surrounded by the darkness of not knowing.

"Are you okay?" Paco was asking.

"What? Yes. I guess."

Her head was aching and her throat gritty. Her heart felt as if it would pound right through her chest. Though she might have died in that burning building, she'd been rescued, and for now that's all that counted, Taffy told herself. Paco was steadying her, large warm hands wrapped around her upper arms. She felt numb except for where he touched her, her responding flesh reminding her that she was alive. She wanted to tell him how much she appreciated what he'd done but, filled with emotions she'd never before experienced, the words stuck in her throat.

And then the chance passed.

Paco's friend rounded up the newly arrived paramedics, who led her over to their unit. One of them asked her questions, checked her pupils for dilation and swabbed the cut on the back of her head with an antiseptic that hurt. Even plagued by pain, Taffy couldn't prevent her attention from wandering, first to the fire, then to her rescuer who stood yards away, and finally to the vision that teased the periphery of her memory.

Lieutenant Sondra King arrived, and Taffy's confusion multiplied as she tried to concentrate on the rapidly issued questions first aimed at the two men—photographer Paco Jones and Endeavors owner Bill Long. She'd thought she'd recognized the man, though they'd never formally met. Paco and Bill told the policewoman what they knew. Then it was Taffy's turn. Bill made his excuses and left for home where he would call his artists and some of the other gallery owners with the bad news.

Sondra King told Paco he could go, too, but he stayed. To listen to her story?

"What were you doing in the building so late, Miss Darling?" the detective asked when she finally turned to Taffy.

"Working. Pulling together last-minute details for the fall gala on Friday." Perched on the open back end of the ambulance, her legs too short to allow her feet to touch the ground, she glanced at the fire. "I guess I don't have that to worry about anymore."

That she didn't even have a job struck her for the first time, and Taffy realized she had plenty of other things to worry about, starting with how she was going to pay her exorbitant rent at the end of the month. What was she going to do now? Though totally inexperienced at working for pay, she'd talked her way into one position because of her background and connections. Who knew if she could manage such a coup again? And there was no way she was going to go to her family for help. Their I-told-you-so's would only make her feel like a failure. Again.

"When did you first realize the building was on fire?"

"When I saw it. I smelled smoke, and I went out into the atrium to investigate." Taffy shuddered at the memory that was oddly clear against the muzzy vision that resurfaced. "It was horrible. I ran down the stairs. Tried not to breathe." Footsteps echoed in her mind. "I was on my way to the front doors when I—I knew I wasn't alone."

"Go on," King urged.

"I don't remember all the details." Taffy was aware of the other woman scribbling in her little notebook, of Paco hanging on her every word. The vision teased her. In her mind, she was moving in slow motion, glancing back over her shoulder. "I—I was trying to get out and saw . . . something moving toward me."

"A person?"

The dark figure. "Yes." Taffy shook her head. A mistake. Her surroundings began to whirl and she squinched in reaction. "Everything is fuzzy now." She put her hand to the back of her head. "He must have hit me with something."

"What did this alleged attacker look like?"

"I only got a glimpse." Taffy shrugged, hating the helpless feeling that threatened to consume her. She was stronger than this. She could take care of herself, no matter what her father said!

"Are you certain there was another person in the building with you?"

Taffy didn't care for the detective's suspicious tone. "What are you intimating? That I was imagining things—or that I'm making this up?"

Sondra King didn't answer. Rather she asked, "Do you have any enemies, Miss Darling?"

"Enemies?"

"Someone who might want to get some kind of revenge against you?"

With each word, Taffy got angrier. "Oh, you mean like Loretta Church? When we were in college, I played a dirty trick on her by mixing sand in her face cleanser. She had that well-scrubbed look for weeks. Maybe *she* got her panty hose in such a twist about it that she decided to do me in after all these years!"

"There's no need to be sarcastic—"

"Isn't there?" Her escalating anger made it more difficult for her to breathe. "You're intimating that either I'm lying or that someone burned down a whole building to kill *me.* Either prospect is ridiculous!"

"Perhaps. For your sake, I—"

"She was attacked," Paco cut in, stepping closer to Taffy. "The paramedics treated her."

"She could have tripped," Sondra King stated, turning her full attention to Paco. "In her hurry to get out."

And Paco was facing down the policewoman as if the two of them were alone. "If you had checked the back of her head, you would know that gash came from some kind of—"

"Wait a minute!" Taffy cried. "Don't the two of you argue over me like I don't exist! Furthermore," she said shrilly, her head and lungs both feeling ready to burst, "just for the record, *I* didn't start that fire!"

The detective remained unruffled by the outburst. "Don't worry, there'll be a thorough investigation."

Furious at the other woman's none-too-subtle implications, Taffy popped off the ambulance and landed on her feet, then swayed when her head went light. Her knees buckled, but a firm arm stopped her from falling.

"*I'm* the victim here, Lieutenant King. Try to keep that in mind." Pulled against Paco's solid warm chest, she tried to free herself.

Not giving her an inch, he said, "This woman should be taken to the hospital."

"No way!" Taffy argued, even though she was feeling terrible.

"You could have a concussion. And you sucked in enough of that smoke to choke a horse."

"I'm not going to any hospital."

No way would she put herself in that vulnerable a position. She could see it now: her parents showing up at the hospital and intimidating the doctor into releasing her in their charge as if she were a child.

"I'm hungry and tired and just want to go home." She turned toward Sondra King. "If you don't have any objections, Lieutenant."

The other woman shrugged. "I know where to find you."

Taffy was about to tell the detective where she could look, when Paco gave her shoulders a warning squeeze and asked, "Are you sure I can't take you to the hospital?"

"The paramedics checked me over. I don't need a hospital."

"I didn't hear them say that."

Before he could ask anyone about it, Taffy moved away from the ambulance and was gratified that, rather than trying to stop her, Paco came with her.

She blithely prattled, "All I need is food and my old nightgown and my own bed."

"You're in no shape to drive."

"I'm not about to. I was thinking about finding a taxi. I walked to work this morning," she explained. "I didn't plan on staying quite so late."

"Leaving earlier would have saved you a lot of trouble."

"And you." Taffy stopped in her tracks. This man had saved her life and here she was being crummy to him. Ashamed of herself, she was totally sincere when she said, "I owe you, Paco Jones."

"You don't owe me anything."

Even though she was ever so grateful and determined that she *would* repay the man somehow, Taffy was too tired to contradict him. She'd save that argument for another day. Moving toward the intersection, trying not to think about how much she hurt outside and in, she wavered on the high heels she normally wore to make her seem taller.

"Whoa." Paco gripped her arm and steadied her again. "You're not going anywhere alone. Forget the taxi, even if you could find one. My car is just down the street."

"But I've put you to enough trouble."

"Don't argue, because you won't win," he stated, sweeping her in the direction he'd indicated. "One question. Once we get to your place, how are you going to get in?" He glanced at the building that was now wreathed in smoke and flame. "I'd say your purse is history."

Taffy wrinkled her brow and moaned. "Great. I didn't even think about that. Do you know what a pain it is to get a new driver's license and replacement credit cards?" Without waiting for an answer, she added, "Don't worry, I can get in."

They hadn't gone but a dozen yards before they were surrounded by media types. Flashes popped off one after the other. Then a brilliant beam clicked on from the top of a television camera, and a reporter shoved a microphone in Taffy's face.

"How did it feel to be trapped in a burning building?" the young man asked.

"Like a marshmallow ready to be roasted." Her tone might be as light as her response, but she was losing patience fast. "What do you think it felt like?"

"Since I've never been involved in a fire, I wouldn't know."

When Taffy was tempted to suggest he could cross the street and find out for himself, she knew she'd passed her stress limit. She wasn't normally a cruel or even a peevish person. But enough was enough, already! Didn't they realize what a trauma she'd just gone through? Why couldn't everyone leave her alone? All she wanted to do was go home and crawl in bed where she would be safe.

Paco must have sensed her increasing torment because he more fully slid his arm around her back. He was attempting to protect her, yet surprisingly—unlike her reaction to her own family—Taffy didn't resent the fact.

"Let the lady be," he told the reporters and photographers calmly but firmly. "Go find someone else to give you your story."

"What about you? Are you the man that rescued her?"

Ignoring the questions thrown at him, Paco shouldered through the small crowd. Free at last, Taffy felt a moment's relief before realizing they were being dogged by a particularly aggressive reporter.

"I only want to ask one more question...."

Without missing a step, Paco growled, "I wouldn't if I were you," with such menace that the guy stopped in his tracks.

Taffy looked at Paco searchingly. He wore an intimidating aura of authority.

Not that *she* was intimidated.

Her emotions about Paco Jones were much more complex. She wanted to know what made him tick. What made him risk his life to save that of a total stranger. What made him take responsibility for her? Well, that wouldn't last long—she could take care of herself. But right now, just for a little while, she would indulge him. She would let him see her safely home.

Taffy held on to her peace of mind until she was inside Paco's car.

That's when the fire vision resurfaced. When the shadowy figure taunted her. For a fleeting second she saw her attacker's face—features cruel and twisted as he came for her—before the vision turned to smoke.

She'd seen the arsonist's face, however briefly. He'd known that. He'd left her for dead because he thought she could identify him. If only she could. If only she could focus her mind's eye more clearly.

Shivering, Taffy huddled down into the passenger seat and wondered if she would ever feel safe again.

As PACO DROVE AWAY from the fire scene, he wondered if it would do any good to pitch the hospital idea one last time. Glancing at his passenger, he doubted it. The rigid set of her chin was an outer indicator of her inner stubbornness. Most people would have collapsed under such pressure and would have let someone else make all the decisions. She didn't seem to need anyone. Even so, irrational as the thought was, Paco couldn't help feeling responsible for her.

"Getting me past those reporters is another thing to thank you for," Taffy said, sounding taut and almost at the breaking point. "I'm not used to having so much gratitude for one person."

Instinctively knowing she didn't like feeling beholden, he said, "Forget it."

"I don't want to forget it. I owe you and I always pay my debts."

Paco wondered how much hard currency a life was worth, for he was certain that's what she meant. He didn't need her money.

Rather than protest, he let the subject drop and followed directions to her place, which was only a short distance from Superior Promenade. Or what would be left of the gallery building in the morning, he thought grimly. He didn't care about the structure itself, but all that artwork lost! So much passion and beauty wiped out by an uncaring, unfeeling entity. Such a waste.

"We're here," Taffy said, indicating a stark redbrick building.

Paco pulled into the loading zone. Formerly an old warehouse near the prestigious East Bank Club, the building had been converted into luxury loft apartments. He'd had no idea a special-events person for a small concern was paid well enough to afford one. Not that she had a job now. He helped Taffy out of the car and followed her to her door.

"I'll come in with you."

She didn't argue, merely nodded and led the way into the vestibule where she punched out a code on a

digital pad. The inner door clicked open. They crossed
to the waiting elevator where she pressed seven. As the
car ascended, Paco wondered if a neighbor had the
key to her apartment or if she was one of those foolish people who hid a spare under the doormat.

"So how are you going to get in?" he asked, thinking she might even have a roommate.

Or a husband.

When she said, "I have a touch-pad security system similar to the one downstairs," he was oddly relieved.

No male here…though that didn't mean she didn't
have one in her life. And what did he care anyway? He
was only seeing that she got home safely.

But when her apartment door opened, Taffy turned
to him, her brown eyes wide. "Listen, why don't you
come in and I'll find us something to eat."

About to tell her he wasn't hungry, Paco changed
his mind. Something in her voice, in her expression,
got to him. She wasn't just asking. She was pleading
without using the words that would make her seem
weak. She obviously didn't want to be alone just yet.
Nor was she willing to admit as much.

"Sure. I could use a snack."

She stepped inside the high-ceilinged room that was
an open space for living and dining areas and kitchen.
"I hope you can wait a few minutes while I get cleaned
up."

He closed the door behind him. "I'll wait."

"Good."

She smiled, the expression sunny and in direct contrast with her soot-smeared face. He'd bet she would
clean up nice.

Taffy raced up the metal spiral staircase, saying, "Beer and wine in the fridge. Help yourself."

"Yeah, sure."

But Paco spent the time prowling her loft, inspecting her modern, pricey if plain furniture that formed a neutral backdrop to an abundance of artwork that represented quite an investment. She could open a gallery herself.

Canvases, watercolors and sculptures of varying sizes had been placed on the walls and in every nook and cranny to the best effect. Everywhere he turned, he found something pleasing to the eye. Taffy Darling was certainly no snob where her taste in artwork was concerned. He recognized many of the artists. Pieces worth barely a hundred dollars were placed side by side with others worth tens of thousands.

No wonder she'd been hired to coordinate special events at Superior Promenade—not that her salary could've bought the items she displayed.

He was captivated by a mixed-media new-age canvas. Fire radiated from behind a woman, who looked into a vessel of burning oil, flames reflected in her eyes. He was thinking it had cost Taffy a fortune when he heard her ask, "Like what you see?"

He whipped around to find Taffy descending the staircase barefoot and drowning in a plush green robe, her wet hair slicked back and held with a clip. He'd been correct. She cleaned up *real* nice.

"I like," he said, not talking about the representation of the woman on the wall.

But his immediate thoughts about Taffy were inappropriate, Paco realized, not only for the situation but because of who they were. He came from poverty while she clearly came from wealth. He should have known it—another spoiled little rich girl playing at a job, taking work from someone who could really use the opportunity to make something of him or herself.

He'd come far from his own ghetto upbringing, was far from poor, thanks to his work in commercial photography, yet he'd never stopped being wary of those born to affluence. He felt more comfortable going back to visit his old neighborhood than he did rubbing shoulders on Chicago's Gold Coast, though he could almost afford to live there himself now.

Taffy couldn't have the faintest idea of what he was thinking, for she stopped next to him and cocked her head as she gazed at the mixed-media piece.

"I bought this at a charity auction last year."

Aware of her fresh clean scent and the natural beauty of her well-scrubbed skin, Paco stirred restlessly and decided he should leave as soon as possible. Though his interest was piqued, he knew she wasn't for him. He'd stick with the models he used in his photographs. They were ambitious young women who worked hard to build themselves a better life, and he could identify with them far more easily than with Taffy Darling.

She indicated the artwork. "It's called *Fire Goddess.*"

Despite himself, he was thoroughly inspecting her turned-up nose, big brown eyes and cupid's-bow mouth. "Lovely," he murmured.

"All of Fiona M's work has a special mystical quality."

Taffy spoke of the painting wistfully. She seemed . . . sad. Or maybe she was just giving in to the emotional trauma she'd been trying to deny since she'd regained consciousness.

"I admire your whole collection, but this one's my favorite," Paco admitted. He didn't like the fact that she so easily had his empathy. Nor did he like how attracted he was to her. "By the way, how are you feeling?"

"As well as can be expected, I guess. I took a couple of aspirin to relieve my pounding head. Hopefully, my throat and chest will feel better in the morning." She wrapped her arms around herself. Then she smiled at him, her expression filled with true rather than fabricated warmth. "But I'm alive and in one piece and that's all that counts, isn't it?"

He was amazed at her upbeat attitude so close on the heels of a brush with death. "You're a lucky lady."

"Yes, I am," she said sincerely, "to have such a brave rescuer."

"Please—"

"Don't. I promise I won't get all gushy. I just want to repay you."

"I don't need your money," Paco growled, satisfied that he found something to be annoyed about.

Her smile faded. "I—I wasn't thinking of money. I meant something more personal. Something I can do or get for you..."

"Nothing. I have everything I need."

"No one has everything." She shook her head and moved toward the kitchen area. "Many cultures believe that if someone saves your life, you're in that person's debt until you return the favor. Since that doesn't seem a likely prospect, I'll have to think of something more creative. In the meantime, I hope an omelet is an appropriate indication of my good intentions. It's one of the things I do really well."

She ran all her words together as if she were afraid he might object yet again. Her underlying vulnerability made her appealing. Everything about her was appealing. He didn't want to stick around to find out exactly how much.

"An omelet would be fine if I were hungry. Truth is, I'd just finished dinner before we spotted the fire."

"Oh." Her disappointment was evident in the single syllable. "Well, what about a cup of coffee?"

"I really should get home." And away from her as soon as possible.

"I'm keeping you." She spoke softly. "I'm sorry. I didn't mean to. I've taken up enough of your time for one night, haven't I?"

Her tone was light, but Paco heard the chagrin beneath the words. Now she was embarrassed. He didn't want her thinking she'd done anything out of line just because he found being around her uncomfortable.

"Time well spent," he assured her. "I don't begrudge a minute of it. But I do have an early location shoot."

"Then I'll see you to the door safely."

Once there, she rose up on her toes and kissed his cheek. All too responsive to the light brush, he stirred. He was tempted to respond in an outward manner, to take her in his arms and kiss her good-night properly. But he would mean goodbye. And so he didn't make a move.

"Take care of yourself, Taffy Darling."

"You haven't seen the last of me, Paco Jones."

Her words danced in his head as he reclaimed his Jeep and drove off into the night. He wouldn't see her again. There was no reason to, unless the arsonist was caught and they both had to testify at the trial.

Paco frowned. He was certain the criminal had tried to kill Taffy to protect his own identity.

What would the arsonist do when he found out Taffy Darling was still alive?

Chapter Three

She was alive!

Reviewing the facts in black and white, he cursed the fates aloud. She was supposed to be dead, not staring out at him from the morning newspaper! She appeared small and helpless next to her savior. Her hair was a tangle around her soot-blackened face—a face he would never forget.

Just as she wouldn't forget his.

He scanned the article for the facts: alleged assailant unnamed. No description...rescued woman couldn't quite remember. Investigating officer suspicious...

Relief flowed through his veins even before he got all the way through the story. The woman the reporter identified as Taffy Darling was not only experiencing some form of traumatic amnesia—it seemed she was herself suspect.

He was safe for the moment.

But what of tomorrow or the day after? What if she remembered then? How long would he be forced to look over his shoulder?

Forever, maybe.

He didn't like that, not one bit. Sloppy work. He should have made certain, not left her death up to fate after she saw his face. But then he wasn't really a murderer. Sometimes, though, circumstances made a man into something he wasn't, made him do things he might never otherwise consider.

He had to protect himself. Had to finish it. But how to find her? He locked on to the face of Paco Jones. Hero of the day. Her rescuer would know where she was. Of that he was certain. He would track her down through the well-known photographer.

He focused on Taffy Darling once more and part of him pitied her.

She had no idea of what she was in for.

TAFFY STARED GLUMLY at the morning newspaper and refused to focus on the picture that reminded her of exactly how close she'd come to losing her life. Superior Promenade had been gutted by the fire. All that was left was the building's skeletal structure, and even parts of that were gone.

Trying not to react emotionally, Taffy skimmed the details of the fire itself, similar to one weeks before in a mid-north area, one of four in the neighborhood torched that summer, possibly by gangs. Police connected the gallery fire to the most recent neighborhood fire because investigators had found traces of burned waxed paper in the rubble of both buildings.

Waxed paper? How frightening that a common household item could be so dangerous.

She read on about the losses. The building's owner was insured. But the entrepreneurs who had put their dreams into their galleries, and the artists who had placed their work in the exhibits, were a different story. The artists especially were devastated. One middle-aged man was quoted as saying he was giving up. After a lifetime of struggle, he'd finally gotten some recognition only to lose everything.

Taffy knew how that felt, not that a job was the same as one's life work. It was just that she, too, was going to have to start over again, to find some way to support herself when she really wasn't qualified to do much. If it hadn't been for her contacts and her experience in working on charity events, she wouldn't have had a prayer at Superior Promenade in the first place. Maybe she could talk her way into another gallery job. In the meantime, she would be forced to sell part of her own collection to keep the wolf from her door.

Depressed at the thought, she went back to her newspaper. She followed the narrative where it continued in the middle of the front section. But before she could pick up on the story, her attention was caught by a connected sidebar that detailed the earlier fires in the Uptown area. Its centerpiece was a photograph of a young Hispanic woman with all the life drained from her. The unidentified teenager had died of smoke inhalation.

Taffy stared in morbid fascination, wondering if she herself had looked so pitiful when Paco found her. Bill Long said she hadn't been breathing, that Paco had given her mouth-to-mouth after rescuing her from the burning building.

No one had been there for the dead girl in the picture.

Taffy shivered and her eyes stung for the unidentified victim. Did no one care enough to wonder what had happened to her? Dead. That could have been her, if not for a man who had been willing to put his life in jeopardy for a total stranger.

Paco Jones was a hero in every sense of the word, and Taffy renewed her vow to repay him somehow... if it was the last thing she ever did.

DESPITE HIS GOOD SENSE, Paco was thinking about Taffy as he parked the Jeep in front of his graystone duplex. He couldn't quite forget the appealing image of the blonde with her hair slicked back from her face and her bare toes peeking out from under her voluminous robe. Not that he would ever get the opportunity to photograph her that way as he wanted to.

"I don't know about you, boss, but I'm pooped," his assistant, Helen Ward, said with a yawn, distracting him from impossible fantasies for a moment.

"Tired already at your age?" It was only early afternoon and Helen was all of twenty-four, a good ten years younger than Paco himself.

"I had a late date." She vigorously scrubbed fingers through her riot of red curls as if trying to stimulate her brain. "I came to work directly from Honky-Tonk," she said, naming her favorite dance club.

Not that he could tell by her clothes since she always wore black. "And I'm supposed to sympathize, huh?" Paco asked as they alighted from the Jeep and walked around to the rear.

Out dancing all night when she knew they had to be down by the lake and ready to start a grueling shoot at sunrise. Paco shook his head. At least the drive back to his place had been short enough so that she hadn't fallen asleep on him. Trying to remember what it had been like to be young, he relented.

"All right, after we get the equipment inside, you can pack it in for the day."

"Ah, boss, you're a peach."

They began pulling bags of expensive equipment from the rear of the vehicle.

So far, his neighborhood was safe if unkempt. But he could imagine Taffy Darling's reaction to it as compared with hers. Not that she was ever going to get the chance.

Noticing Helen was loaded down with equipment bags, he asked, "Can you carry all that?"

"If it'll save me a second trip up those stairs, you bet I can. As long as you unlock the door for me."

She rushed to the front steps, Paco following with more bags, attached to which were light stands and a tripod.

From the outside, his graystone looked as worn as its few neighbors, but Paco had gutted the inside and transformed it into a combination work and living space that would match anything on the Gold Coast. He ran his business from the first floor and lived on the second. Seven large rooms provided far too much space for a single man and two cats, but after growing up in overcrowded conditions, he appreciated the luxury.

In the vestibule, he unlocked the door that led them into the small first-floor reception area. "After we unpack, bring the exposed rolls of film into the darkroom," Paco told Helen. "I'll develop them later." He found it unnecessary and a waste of time and money to bring film to a lab when he shot in black and white.

They crossed through the studio where several sets were currently ready for photo shoots.

"You don't have to do my job, boss. I promise I'll be here bright and early in the morning."

"You're taking the day off tomorrow, remember?" Besides which, he needed to be busy so he wouldn't keep thinking about the fire...or about a certain blonde.

"Well, if you insist..."

Helen stopped mid-sentence and midstride a few feet inside the large open space that served as office, work area and equipment storage room. Several folders lay on the floor, contact sheets spilling out of them. She quickly set down the equipment bags near the wall of locked cabinets and got busy straightening up the mess.

"You should keep those monsters upstairs where they belong," she muttered, her voice tight.

"I didn't purposely let the cats come downstairs this morning, but maybe one of the little beggars sneaked out when I wasn't looking. Phantom?" Paco called. "Peaches?"

No responding meow came from some hidey-hole. But if one of the cats hadn't knocked over the folders, who had?

"Seems they're not guilty, after all."

"Or one of them managed to get down here, mess up the place and get back upstairs," Helen said.

As she set the work back on the table where it belonged, Paco looked around, his gaze intent, for anything else out of place. He couldn't be certain, but he

thought the top of his desk was messier than he remembered. He scanned the folders and papers covering the surface and got the oddest feeling that
something wasn't right.

"Can I borrow your keys a minute?" Helen asked,
sounding odd. When he handed them to her, she unlocked the cabinets and began unpacking bags in silence. Usually she chattered incessantly. Did she feel
the same way, then?

A chill of warning shot up Paco's spine. Instinctively he went to the filing cabinets and opened a
drawer. A clunk claimed his attention. He whirled
around to see Helen grabbing a lens before it could hit
the floor. The piece of equipment was worth more
than a thousand dollars and it wasn't like his assistant
to be so careless.

"Hey, keep your mind on what you're doing," he
demanded. "What's the matter with you, anyway?"

She kept her back to him. "I told you I was tired."

But Paco sensed her sudden attack of the clumsies
came from nerves, not lack of sleep. He didn't challenge her, merely scanned file folders of contact sheets
and photographs as she continued putting things away.
When his commercial work proved to be in order, he
went on to the drawer containing his personal photographs. His growing tension seemed well-founded as
he skimmed through the files.

"Have you been in here lately?" he asked.

"What?"

"My personal photographs. Have you been reor-
ganizing them or something?"

Helen continued to empty the equipment cases.
"No."

"*Someone* has been going through them."

Reluctantly, he thought, she met his direct gaze. "Right. Like Peaches or Phantom were looking for pictures you took of them."

"Don't be so flippant, Helen. I know how I had my photos organized—by subject. Things are out of place. Some prints seem to be missing."

She shifted her gaze away from him. "You've had a tough week, boss. I'm sure things will sort themselves out eventually."

Thoughtfully he closed the drawer. "Never mind," he said. "I'm sure you're right—I must have misplaced them."

"Probably."

She rapidly shoved several more lenses onto their shelves. Was she really as nervous as he thought? Or was he projecting?

"Listen, boss, I can't stay on my feet another minute longer," she said, her tone clipped. "I've got to go home and get horizontal, like now. Okay?"

Paco stared. Her face was pale, making her freckles more prominent. And her eyes were shadowed. With fatigue? Fright? Guilt? He didn't know which.

"Yeah, go home. I'll finish up here."

"Thanks," she muttered, making for the door without looking back. "See you Friday, then."

"Early," he added.

But she was already gone.

And Paco was left with the growing suspicion that something bizarre was going on.

Only—what?

TAFFY DIDN'T KNOW why she had such a persistent streak. She guessed it ran in the family she was so reluctant to turn to in time of need. Persistence was what brought her to Paco Jones's office that afternoon. Inside the vestibule, she tried the door. Locked. She pressed the doorbell to his apartment and hoped he was at home.

Anxiety pressed her until she heard her voice over the intercom. "Who's there?"

"It's Taffy. Taffy Darling," she clarified as though she shared the first name with hordes of other women.

"Just a minute."

The words were as curt as his tone. Paco did not sound pleased by her arrival. Taffy bit her lip. Maybe she'd made a mistake. Maybe she'd better leave. About to take her offering of thanks and go home, she changed her mind yet again when she heard his quick tread on the stairs. The door flung open and he stood there, glaring at her, his expression intimidating.

Only Taffy reminded herself that he couldn't intimidate *her*.

"What is it?" he demanded, sounding suspicious.

"I brought you something." She indicated the carefully wrapped package that stood waist-high between them.

He didn't even give it so much as a glance. His black eyes locked with hers as he demanded, "How did you know where to find me?"

Now she was getting annoyed. "Why don't you invite me in and I'll tell you?"

He cocked his head toward the stairs, then spun around and took them two at a time. Taffy struggled her way up to the second floor, careful that the package didn't catch on anything. How rude! The least he could have done was offer to carry it since she'd brought the darned thing for him!

Paco was waiting for her at the top of the stairs, his arms crossed over his broad chest. He was wearing a bloodred shirt with black embroidery both at the cuffs and along the open-throated collar. He looked incredibly masculine despite the unusual garment.

Her pulse trilled as she thrust the package at him. "For you."

Reluctantly he unfolded his arms and took the offering. "What is it?"

"Don't you have any manners at all?" Taffy demanded, now truly sorry that she'd ever left home.

He seemed about to argue with her. Then his expression changed. "Sorry. I shouldn't be taking my bad mood out on you."

"It's that piece you were admiring last night. *Fire Goddess.*"

He frowned. "I can't take something so valuable."

"Not as valuable as my life is to me."

"You can't put a price on a human life."

"You're right," she said, wondering why he was being so harsh with her. "This is just a token."

"But there's no reason for you to give away something you yourself love."

"Yes there is—I want to."

Taffy was getting frustrated. She couldn't repay Paco in kind, so she was doing the next best thing. The best she knew how. But as she'd heard too many times in her life, her best just wasn't good enough. Her father particularly had tried to drill that into her head.

"Come in," Paco finally offered, surprising her. "We can talk about it."

He even held the door for her.

The interior of Paco's apartment was a sleekly modern, expensively decorated study in black and white. High-gloss white walls, black leather furniture in the living room, black veneer table and wall unit in the dining room. Zebra-striped area rugs covered the central portions of both shiny wooden floors, and living room pillows and dining room chairs were covered with matching print.

But the fascinating thing about the rooms was the black-and-white framed photographs on the walls.

Taffy approached the closest one, a shot of a woman and her child on the street, standing next to a shopping cart loaded with filled plastic bags. Homeless. Taffy swallowed hard and inspected another of three little girls jumping rope in front of a run-down liquor store and a drunk asleep on the sidewalk. Powerful pictures that told their own stories.

"Are these your work?"

"Those two are," he agreed. "And a few others. I also collect pieces by half a dozen other photographers I admire."

Realizing how out of place her new-age artwork would be in his apartment, Taffy murmured, "Oops, I goofed." She pointed at the package still in his hands. "I thought you really liked the Fiona M. piece."

His black brows lifted. "I do like it."

"But it's not your taste, right, and it doesn't fit here. Of course I understand." She was speaking so quickly out of embarrassment that her words were running together. "Though I really did want you to have it. I was just trying to make good on my promise."

Sighing, Paco set the piece of artwork against a wall. "Since you won't feel like you're off the hook until you give me some tangible thanks, I accept. Now we're even."

"No we're not, but it was the best I could do."

Taffy couldn't believe she'd said that. Waiting for a responding criticism, she was pleased when none followed. Now what? She'd accomplished what she'd come for, right? So what was she doing, standing around and twiddling her thumbs like some teenager.

"Maybe you'd like to sit," he suggested, indicating the grouping around the fireplace.

"Um, I guess I shouldn't bother you any longer."

"You're not bothering me," he said, surprising her yet again. He took her arm and led her toward the couch. "Really. I was in a bad mood before you ever got here."

Taffy plopped down, asking, "Want to talk?" The offer was out of her mouth before she had the good sense to think about it.

Paco sat in the chair next to her. "Let's start with how you found me."

"That was easy. I called Joel Rubin, the guy in charge of the company that manages . . . rather, that managed Superior Promenade." It was still difficult for Taffy to believe the gallery building was gone. "He gave me Bill Long's number. And Bill gave me your address when I told him why I needed it."

Silent for a moment, he seemed as if he were deciding on something. "I probably should explain my grouchiness," he finally said. "I suspect an unknown party got into my office downstairs and removed some of my best prints."

Goose bumps crawled along Taffy's arms. First the fire. Now a possible break-in. Too weird to be a co-incidence? "Uh, maybe you misplaced a few photographs."

"Yeah, that's what my assistant thinks. I was planning on double-checking, but I doubt I'll find them."

"Have you called the police?"

He gave her another one of his dark looks and laughed. The harsh sound grated on her nerves. "That would be a joke. I grew up in the ghetto. I've had my share of run-ins with the cops. I'm not about to make friends with them now."

Taffy didn't know how to respond to his statement. She was out of her depths when it came to illegal activities and dealing with the police. She'd never even been the victim of a crime before the fire. Now it seemed Paco was a victim, if in a less direct manner than she. If those prints really *were* missing. They'd both been through a lot in the past twenty-four hours, and she wouldn't be surprised if his judgment was affected just a bit.

"Why don't I help you look for those prints, Paco. You said you were going to double-check, right?"

Though he gave her an exasperated expression, he growled, "Come on," as he crossed to the door.

Taffy jumped up and followed him down the stairs. "So do you have a theory as to why someone might steal your work?"

Paco unlocked the office door. The walls of the reception area were hung with his commercial photography, from a brochure for a trucking company to a Christmas advertisement for a local department store.

"Not for their value."

Taffy was slightly distracted by the various sets in the studio. In one corner was a complete modern kitchen. Another corner was draped with gauzy materials and loaded with pillows like a room in a harem.

"Maybe we can figure it out together," she said, still looking around.

Paco stopped short. "We?"

But Taffy headed straight into the office. "Together...assuming they are missing. You still have all your negatives, though, don't you?"

"I keep them in a wall safe."

"Good thinking."

After a quarter of an hour of searching the place, Taffy was about to admit defeat. She closed a folder of contact sheets and placed it back on the table with the others. In doing so, she knocked over a marking pen, then stooped to retrieve it. A flash of something red nestled between the table leg and wall caught her eye.

She reached for it. A soft piece of material— She straightened with it in her hand.

And froze.

The recurring vision flashed through her mind, clearer this time. Her memory was returning. While flames blazed around her, an angry face loomed close. Try as she would, she couldn't make out the features clearly.

What she did see was a sweatband with the initials "L.L."—exactly like the one she was holding in her hand!

Chapter Four

"Maybe they *are* connected, after all," Taffy said, her back to Paco.

"What are connected?" he asked.

"The two incidents. Two crimes," she amended. "The fire and now a theft. How bizarre." Turning, she held out her fist and Paco caught a glimpse of red between fingers squeezed so tight the knuckles were turning white in contrast. "*He* was wearing one of these."

Paco was irritated and not in the mood for guessing games, but when he noticed her face unusually pale and drawn, he held his temper in check. "Who was?"

"The man in the gallery who tried to k-kill me." Her voice broke. "I—I remember seeing it."

Her eyes squinched into slits, and Paco knew she was looking inward now. Searching. He could feel the tension surrounding her. Then she let out a heart-rending cry of frustration and her expression changed to one of anger.

"If only I could remember everything clearly. But it's just coming back in bits and pieces."

"Let me see what you've got there." Paco stepped closer, and when she didn't move, he wrapped his hand around her smaller fist and gently pried open her stiff fingers. Touching her distracted him for a moment. But what lay revealed in her hand shocked him into forgetting about his attraction to the blonde and sent his heart plummeting. He picked up the band of cloth and examined it more closely. "'L.L.'—Latin Lovers."

"What's that?" she asked. "A music group?"

"A gang."

Her eyes widened and she swallowed hard. "You're kidding, aren't you?"

She couldn't possibly be that innocent—gangs were a fact of life in any metropolis. "Where'd you grow up? In Disney World?"

"Um, North Shore, both Winnetka and Kennilworth," Taffy mumbled as if she were embarrassed at having to admit she was from the ritzy northern suburbs lining Lake Michigan rather than from the inner city. "So you think some gang started that fire and then stole your prints?"

"Not necessarily. I shot photos of gang members for my personal collection," Paco quickly stated, though he feared that's exactly what might have happened. "One of them could have dropped the sweatband here."

He knew he was rationalizing. That would be practically impossible since he'd taken the photographs in Latin Lovers' territory, not in his studio. Only one gang member had been free to come and go at will....

"Is that what you really think?" Taffy asked, breaking into Paco's dark thoughts.

"No. I don't believe in coincidences," he admitted honestly.

Not that he had to tell her the whole truth. If Ramon were involved in illegal activities, Paco would personally break his scrawny little neck! He'd warned his younger brother about the gangs, but his lectures had fallen on deaf ears. No one had been able to stop Ramon from signing up, not even his father—Paco's stepfather—Tito Marquez. Paco had all the respect in the world for Tito. It was to the older man's credit that Paco had become a successful photographer rather than an inmate at Joliet State Prison as several of his friends and acquaintances had. Tito had been the best thing ever to happen to Paco and his mother Rose.

If only Tito's own children, Ramon and Marita, Paco's half siblings, respected their father's opinion half as much as Paco did.

"Are you all right?"

The question cut through the stomach-churning thoughts that were filling Paco's head. He looked down at Taffy, who seemed to have recovered from her shock quite nicely. Color washed her face once more, though her expression was fixed in concern—for him, he knew, rather than for herself.

Uncomfortable under her close scrutiny, he moved away. "I'll look into this," he said, indicating the sweatband. "The person who lost this might have had some connection with the fire." *Must* have, he thought.

"I'll help you."

"No."

"Why not?" she demanded.

"I don't want to see you hurt." Nor did he want to be close enough long enough to get involved with her.

"Thanks so much for your concern, but if you remember correctly, someone already tried to *kill* me! I have a vested interest in finding out who."

And he didn't want her help because Ramon might be involved. He would take care of his half-brother himself. "You'll only get in the way."

"Baloney!"

"Then I'll have to rescue you again," Paco said tersely, knowing he wasn't being fair, but not above doing whatever was necessary to dissuade her.

"I'm perfectly capable of taking care of myself."

"Is that why I had to pull you out of a burning building?"

"If you're trying to make me angry, you're doing a great job. But guess what? The guy who left me to die makes me even angrier!"

She looked furious—her cheeks were flushed, her eyes glittering, her breast was heaving—and exciting. Paco reminded himself noticing was all right. Any more personal thoughts were inappropriate.

"Listen, I'm sorry," he said, trying to smooth things over. "I didn't mean to put those sparks in your cute little eyes." He used a different tactic. "I was just trying to make you realize that this wasn't the kind of situation a woman like you would really want to get involved in."

"Cute little eyes? A woman like me?" Taffy's tone reflected a deep-seated resentment that Paco suspected hadn't begun with him. "That's the problem, isn't it? Look, let's get something straight up front, all right? It's not my fault that you have a chip on your shoulder, so whatever life has dealt you, don't take it out on me."

"I don't have a chip—"

"Firewood," she interrupted. "A big, fat piece of firewood right there."

She angrily poked his shoulder so hard she almost made him take a step back. "Hey!"

"Hey, yourself!"

"Look, Taffy, your intentions are good, but you're out of your league here," he snapped, her anger feeding his.

"Who says?"

"I do. Ever been in the inner city?" When she didn't answer, merely stared at him with lips pressed tight, he said, "I didn't think so. You spend your time on the North Shore or Gold Coast or in the River North area. You wouldn't know how to act around people who weren't born with silver spoons in their mouths."

"I'm not intimidated by you—"

"I'm a pussycat compared to the man who left you for dead."

"Not to mention a reverse snob."

Paco took a deep breath. One of them had to stay rational. "Arguing isn't getting us anywhere."

"No, it isn't, so why don't you shove your prejudices and judge me as a person. I'm not a pampered socialite. Anymore," she added.

She'd hit the problem right on the nose, of course. No matter how appealing or how nice she was, Paco did view Taffy Darling as a spoiled little rich girl unable to relate to the underbelly of the city where he grew up. Spoiled and stubborn. They glared at each other and he knew she wasn't about to give up.

Quickly mulling over the situation, Paco figured he'd better humor the headstrong woman. It wouldn't hurt anything to keep her on the fringes of his own investigation in case she could supply information he needed.

"And given some time and memory jogging," she was going on, "I might even be able to recognize the guy who torched Superior Promenade."

"All right."

"All right?"

She looked taken aback, as if she couldn't believe she'd won so easily. Not that she really had, he thought. But she needn't know that. Paco congratulated himself on his cleverness. He could make her happy using a little pretense, even if that meant he had to send her on a wild-goose chase or two to keep her out of his hair.

And out of his thoughts.

"You win." His purposeful grin met her suspicious expression. "All this energy fighting each other could be turned into something more positive."

"So we start with the photographs, right?" He nodded his agreement and the suspicion gradually faded. "They have to be the connection."

"Exactly what I was thinking," Paco told her, agreeable now that he'd figured out how to handle her. "First I have to go through my files again to see which copies are missing. Then I'll duplicate those prints, though I'm not sure where that'll get us. I'll let you know if I get any ideas."

"You want me to leave?"

Hoping to assuage any remaining suspicions, he kept his tone reasonable. "What good would your staying do? Are you qualified to be a lab assistant?"

"Qualified?" she echoed in a small voice. "No, I've never worked in a darkroom before, but if you would just give me a chance—"

"Then the best thing you can do is go home and get a good night's sleep," he interrupted before she could push her services on him. "I promise I'll keep in touch."

"If you don't, I know where to find you," she threatened.

"Fair enough."

"And if you're humoring me, *don't,*" she muttered as she swept by him. "I don't give up so easily."

"Tell me something I don't already know."

She didn't bother with a retort but headed straight for the door that would lead her back out onto the street. He waited until it closed behind her before he picked up the phone and dialed his family's number. He stared at the sweatband while the phone rang.

No answer.

His mother and Tito would be busy working in the small grocery store they ran, of course, but he'd hoped Marita or Ramon himself would answer. Ramon had always been a good kid, but a good kid could turn bad fast once seduced by gang mentality. No doubt his seventeen-year-old brother was hanging out with those compatriots who would sooner or later bring his whole family grief.

Paco only hoped it wouldn't be sooner, for, no matter how much he'd prefer avoiding the cops altogether, he couldn't allow a serious crime to go unpunished. He could overlook the theft of his own work, but what if that led back to the fire and the attempt on Taffy Darling's life as he suspected?

There was no getting around it—Paco feared he was about to set in motion his own brother's first serious set-to with the law.

The doorbell suddenly buzzed, jarring him. Had Taffy forgotten something or had she come back to threaten him some more?

Not in the mood for more, he trudged to the entrance, but when he swung the door open, he faced Gilbert Koroneos, Luce Sandoval's hotshot press assistant, dressed as usual in a pale suit with a brilliantly patterned shirt. Also as usual he wore no tie, and the first three buttons of his shirt were unfastened, revealing a thick gold chain.

"Gilbert. What can I do for you?"

"Actually, I'm not here to see you. I told Helen I'd pick her up after work." Gilbert made a fake smoothing motion to his already slicked-back hair, the kind of thing teenaged boys used to signal they'd scored. "We, uh, had a late night last night and I said I'd make it up to her."

"Helen went home early."

Paco regretted his assistant was dating the oily front man. Helen and Gilbert had met when Paco had taken publicity stills for both Luce and David. Brother and sister had run against each other in the last election until it became clear that Luce had the voters enthralled. Then David had withdrawn. Once Luce had been elected, she'd talked David into joining her team and working with her in an unofficial capacity.

Gilbert passed Paco, not seeming discouraged that Helen wasn't around. "Listen, I read about the fire. So you're a real live hero now, huh?"

"Forget hero. Good citizen will do."

"Ah, come on. Someone should pin a medal on you for saving the blonde." He knuckled Paco in the arm, making Paco want to knuckle him back... in the mouth. "Now, if you had a publicist," Gilbert went on, "someone looking out for your best interests, you could milk this story and get all kinds of new clients."

"I don't need a publicist."

Especially not one like Gilbert Koroneos. He resented the other man telling him how to run his business. He couldn't fathom why Luce had ever hired the guy in the first place. Of course Gilbert had helped her get elected. He was good at what he did. That didn't mean Paco had to like him.

"While I'm here, I figured you and me, we could talk," Gilbert was saying.

"About?"

"A little public-relations work Luce wants to do. She's going to carry out her campaign promises unlike a lot of politicians."

"Good. How does that involve me?"

"You're a photographer. Luce told me you had some pretty dynamite prints in your show, some taken in our ward. Sorry about the loss, but you got copies or negatives or something, right?"

The prints again! "Something," Paco said noncommittally, wondering what Gilbert was driving at.

"Well, we were talking about it, Luce and David and me. We thought about using a few of those shots in the next ward newsletter. Kinda like a 'See what's going on in our neighborhood' photo essay. You know, to inspire the good citizens of the ward to get organized against crime and violence.''

Paco trusted the press assistant the least when he was at his most sincere. "Whose idea exactly was this?''

"I'd like to take credit, but David came up with the idea. He and I, we don't always get along, but I have to back him on this one. It could be good for Luce.''

"Tell her I'll think about it.''

"You do that.'' Gilbert started to leave, but paused in the doorway. "So Helen what—went home?''

Paco nodded. "Said she wanted to get horizontal right away.''

Gilbert grinned, revealing his gold fillings. "Then I'd better get right over there fast. See you around, Paco.''

Not if Paco could help it.

Locking the door behind the departing press assistant, Paco was thoughtful. Why was everyone so interested in those damn prints?

He decided it was high time he found out.

WHILE RUNNING several errands before returning home, Taffy alternately felt satisfaction that she'd gotten her way with Paco Jones and despair at actually having to work with him. Just what she needed— getting involved with a reverse snob. She was thinking she should have her head examined as she exited her cleaners, arms loaded.

She'd parked her car at the other end of the block, near a fire hydrant. She'd only been gone a few minutes, but sure enough, a bright orange ticket decorated the windshield of her even brighter red MG.

"Darn!"

She opened the sports car and set her cleaning inside, then took the ticket and threw it with the others piled on the floor in front of the passenger's seat.

By the time she got behind the wheel, her mind was already back on Paco. It wasn't too late. She could call the police herself and let them know about the theft of his prints. But just thinking about talking to Lieutenant King one more time than necessary set her on edge. Besides, as she'd insisted to Paco, she did have a vested interest in finding the person who'd left her for dead. She'd love to be the one to put the bastard behind bars!

Wouldn't that show her family she could be competent at something?

She sped away from the cleaners and headed for home, making a right turn on red though a sign forbade her from doing so at this corner.

For too long, people had underestimated her, primarily men, and especially her father. She'd been looked upon with amused tolerance because she was small and cute and rich. Well, the last certainly no longer applied, not that Paco needed to know the details of her circumstances.

All her life, she'd hated being thought of as a stereotype. She'd hated proving people right when they made assumptions about her. And yet she'd fed into that kind of thinking for years and years, more out of rebellion than because of incompetence. Though she wasn't trained for a career, she was smart and she was tougher than anyone gave her credit for. Anyone but

Eden Payne Lovett, her best friend and former roommate. Taffy had come through for Eden when the other woman had been in trouble a couple of years back. So she could certainly come through for herself!

That settled, Taffy felt more at ease. She could do anything if she set her mind to it. All she needed was a chance. Paco was going to give her that opportunity, and she would show him that she was a woman he could depend on.

She was concentrating on her positive mental attitude when she arrived home. Maybe that's why she got lucky and found a parking space directly in front of her building. A legal one. Armed with her cleaning and some things she'd picked up at a drugstore, she entered and checked her mailbox. Stuffed. Without looking to see how many more bills had arrived that she would now have trouble paying, she shoved everything into the plastic bag that held her toiletries and headed for her apartment.

Inside, the red light of her answering machine blinked at her—furiously, Taffy thought. She hit the message button and purposely kept herself busy putting things away as she listened.

"Taffy, why didn't you call and let us know what happened to you?" her mother asked. "How humiliating that I had to find out from your Aunt Agnes who heard about it from Cousin Julia who read about the fire in this morning's *Tribune!*"

"That's the way, Mother. Think of how this'll affect *you,* as usual," Taffy said as the message went on in the same vein. "Don't express any concern over your daughter's welfare or anything."

"Oh . . . I do hope you'll have recovered from that smoke-inhalation thing by Friday because I want you to come to dinner," Nancy Darling continued speaking on the recorder. "We're having the Tylers, and Arthur is looking forward to seeing you."

Taffy took a deep breath as a beep signaled the end of that message. Her mother was still trying to fix her up with the stuffed-shirt son of her best friend. And she must have planned this dinner party days or even weeks ago, despite the fact that Taffy had told her whole family about the opening at Superior Promenade that was so important to her. It was too much to think they might have supported her by attending.

"Taf, are you hiding out or what?" came the voice of her older sister Bitsy Darling Upchurch. "Come on, pick up the phone," she wheedled. Pause. "Okay, so you're not there. Well, call me. I'd sure like to know how you got yourself into *this* mess!"

That was Bitsy—always assuming Taffy had done something inappropriate to get herself into trouble.

"Taffy Elaine, this is your father."

"As if I wouldn't recognize your voice," she muttered, now in the kitchen area where she took a can of soup from a cupboard for dinner.

"Enough is enough. You could have been killed in that fire, for heaven's sake! Now you don't have a job and you don't have any money. When are you going to admit you just can't get along on your own?"

Taffy slammed the can down on the counter. "Never!" Furious, she attacked the metal with the opener.

Her hands betrayed her and the half-open can of soup went scooting across the counter only to dump over on its side. As the contents spilled from the can, so did the tears from her eyes. She hadn't cried after she'd so closely escaped death or anytime thereafter. But now she couldn't control herself. Only her family could do this to her....

"Taffy, darling, it's me." Eden's worried voice cut through the fog of melancholy enveloping her. "We stopped by earlier, but you weren't there. You'd better be all right, because I'm not in the market for a new best friend. Please call so I can breathe easier, okay? And let us know if you need anything. Chick sends his love."

Taffy wiped the tears from her cheeks. Eden and her new husband Chick Lovett cared about her and believed in her even if her own family didn't. Not everyone in the world was convinced she was a thoughtless harebrained incompetent. Her easily hurt feelings temporarily assuaged, she cleaned up the spilled soup and opened another can. She made the call to Eden while dinner was warming, and a few minutes later she was sipping at the hot liquid and sorting through the mail.

Bill. Bill. Advertisement. Magazine. Another bill.

A plain white envelope with only her name neatly typed across the front.

Taffy frowned. No address. No stamp. This hadn't come through the mail. Someone had dropped it in her box. It could be a notice of some sort from the landlord—but then the envelope would be one with the management company's logo. Tearing it open, Taffy quickly pulled out a plain piece of paper and scanned the typed contents.

Taffy—
Found something important that I want you to
see. Meet me at ten tonight, at 4728 N. Green-
way.

                                              Paco

How odd. Why would Paco want her to meet him
someplace she'd never been? Not exactly a choice
neighborhood, either, especially not for a woman
alone at night. Not that she'd ever stepped foot in the
area, no matter the time. And Paco knew that, too.
Remembering their disagreement earlier, she suspected he was testing her. He probably didn't think a
''woman like her'' would show. If she didn't, he would
use the fact in his argument against her helping him.
She should have realized he'd backed down far too
easily!

Knowing and hating that her self-esteem rode on
Paco's acceptance of her as a competent person, Taffy
decided she would be at the given address early!

SHE WAS PROPERLY SPOOKED by the neighborhood
that appeared near deserted and appropriately eerie.
She *was* out of her depths. Okay, she admitted it to
herself even if she had no intentions of giving Paco the
satisfaction of knowing he'd correctly pegged her type.

She hadn't been expecting much of the area, but it
was even more run-down than she had imagined. The
large brick apartment buildings lining the street
needed attention that went much further than the
sprucing up of a coat of paint slapped to peeling window frames and doorways. Many of the lower sur-
faces were covered with graffiti, mostly spray-painted

messages from one gang to another. Even the grounds reflected the almost criminal lack of care of the neighborhood.

A debris-filled vacant lot shouldered the apartment house next to the one where she waited. Beyond that stood an abandoned building, front entrance and both basement and first-floor windows boarded up. Several streetlights were out of order as was the hall light here.

Thankful for the flashlight on her key ring that had allowed her to see the building's address, she waited outside rather than in the vestibule itself.

But as she stood alone, Taffy had the growing feeling that something was terribly wrong. Paco might be a little pigheaded and macho, but he didn't seem to be a cruel man. She couldn't believe he'd want her to be cooling her heels in an area that not only scared the stuffing out of her, but that appeared truly dangerous.

Where was Paco, anyway? She checked her watch as she'd probably done once a minute. Five after ten and she'd been waiting for a quarter of an hour.

In that time, she'd seen few people around. Several noisy teenagers had swaggered down the block, beer cans in hand. An elderly couple had exited a car across the street and had scurried into their building. A lone middle-aged woman had crossed her path, eyes cautiously darting in every direction until she reached her destination.

Despite the temperate breezy September night, Taffy felt chilled to the bone. By contrast, her palms were sweaty. She rubbed them on her draped designer trousers in an effort to control her nerves, but her stomach was knotted and she was finding it increasingly difficult to breathe normally. Each minute dragging by served to convince Taffy that she was playing the fool by waiting. A police siren wailed closer and closer, stretching her nerves taut.

Retrieving the note from her pocket, she used her flashlight to reread the typed message.

Typed. Even Paco's name.

Why hadn't he signed it?

Her unease increased and she made up her mind—she wouldn't wait one second longer.

But as she set off for her car parked on the next block, Taffy had the uncanny feeling that she was being watched by unfriendly eyes. She spun around and a gust of wind shot another chill through her. Walking backward, she scanned the area, but it was so dark. If someone was hiding in a doorway or next to a tree or behind a bush, how would she even know?

She turned and walked faster, her senses fine-tuned to every sound and movement of the night. A scrabble and a dark streak close to the pavement made her jump. A cat. Just a cat, she told herself, her pulse steadying.

Then a sound behind her made by no cat alerted her to another human presence!

Chapter Five

Not running as instinct bade her do was the hardest choice Taffy ever made, considering the footsteps behind her steadily echoed her own. In an attempt to appear naive of any danger, she slid a casual glance over her shoulder and caught the dark silhouette of a man, hands shoved into jacket pockets, covered head down, chin practically tucked into his chest. She was unable to make out any concrete details, merely gathered impressions in that quick analysis. She thought him to be of average height and build.

And, though he gave no outward sign, she sensed he meant her harm. She felt invisible tentacles slither through the night, coming for her, smothering her....

Think! What to do? Her car was too far away to reach quickly. She was walking along the vacant lot. But even if it was an inhabited building, would she be wise to seek shelter there? How could she be certain what waited inside might not be as dangerous as the man following her?

Her gaze skipped over a pile of trash to the abandoned building just ahead. All openings low enough to reach were boarded up securely. What about the back? Wondering if there might be a way in, she swallowed hard at the thought of entering the structure alone.

She'd read about gangs and drug dealers taking over such buildings.

But the man following her was her only reality....

His footsteps speeding up fractionally made her think faster and more recklessly than she might otherwise. Clumps of tall, sad-looking bushes surrounded the front of the next occupied apartment building. She quickened her pace and at the last minute smoothly turned onto the interior sidewalk as if heading toward the doorway, then ducked through a gap in the bushes before the man following her was close enough to actually see what she was doing. The hedge neatly swallowed Taffy, giving her hope of escape.

Inching her way through the living maze toward the back of the building, she listened closely. The footsteps slowed, then stopped as if her pursuer were confused. A muttered curse was followed by his racing to the front door, throwing it open and entering the vestibule.

And Taffy made her escape!

Praying he would investigate the hallway long enough for her to get out of his hearing range, she raced along the gangway, thanking heaven she was wearing heels with soft soles that hushed her footfalls. She flew down several steps, passed the basement entrance and continued up another short flight that brought her to the postage-stamp-sized backyard. If she was lucky, her pursuer would think she'd vanished into thin air... though she knew he would search for her anyway.

And so, when she got to the alley, she didn't stop, merely rounded the garbage bins in back and made for the abandoned building next door.

She was breathing heavily by the time she made it to what was left of the back porch. Under the muted orange glow of a distant alley light, she could see the outside stairwell was a death trap, one she only hoped she could conquer. Squeezing through the two-by-fours that were useless as a deterrent, she avoided sagging boards, gaping holes and completely missing steps all the way up to the second landing. The railing wobbled beneath her hand and she swore the steps did, too. Unbelievable that some city inspector hadn't had the structure torn down.

She'd reached the second landing before she heard her pursuer's footsteps echoing along the building next door, his curse low and violent.

She slid into the shadows.

Hugging the brick wall, she took shallow quiet breaths and waited. The crash of a garbage can told her of his anger. And then he was running in the opposite direction as if determined to find her and end it once and for all.

End what? Her life?

Frightening thoughts whirled in her head as she checked for a way into the building. He wouldn't give up easily, not after going to such trouble to trick her into coming. When he didn't find her, he would realize she hadn't gone on in the other direction.

Then he would be back to search for her here.

Her tiny key-ring flashlight gave her just the illumination she needed to find a loose board covering one of the two back doorways. The door itself stood half-open, and it swung inward on broken hinges, making it obvious that someone had preceded her. Hopefully not tonight. Please God, not tonight.

Taffy slipped through the opening with ease, for once glad of her small size, and pulled the board back in place. The smell that greeted her was rank. Her flashlight revealed the hulk of a kitchen littered with garbage. From the last legal occupants or transients? she wondered. Covering her nose and mouth against the stench, she crossed the debris-littered floor. Something scurried over her foot!

Taffy jumped. Rats! She gulped and moved faster. Hopefully the creatures confined their nocturnal activities to the kitchen area.

A noise from the alley alerted her. Someone was out there. Maybe her pursuer was even now coming for her. She had to find someplace to hide. Whipping from room to room, she tried to make up her mind.

What corner, what closet would be safest? What if she wouldn't be safe at all?

Negative thinking wouldn't get her anywhere, and so with trepidation, Taffy continued her search. A small door close to the floor in the bathroom caught her eye. A laundry chute! The door was sealed shut. She rounded the corner and went into the master bedroom. Another such door sat in the wall opposite the first. This one she pried open.

Her flashlight showed her she was in luck. Someone had sealed off the opening in the floor by covering it with a plank. She climbed inside by tucking herself into a tight ball. Closing the door behind her, she prayed her pursuer wouldn't think about the laundry chute as a possible hiding place. Maybe he wouldn't even spot it.

Within minutes, she heard him moving around on the floor below, muffled clunks reverberating up the shaft. Footsteps, doors opening, something knocked over. Nothing. She began to sweat. Was he coming up here then, intending to search until he found her? Or might he have devised a more clever method of ridding himself of her?

Remembering the fire, she felt a growing sense of panic. What if he figured out she was somewhere in this building, and rather than taking the time to search, torched it to rid himself of her?

Staring into the dark, she could feel the flames searing her, and for a moment, she saw him looming over her again. Dark hair, gang sweatband. What else? Why couldn't she see his face?

Then the vision dissipated, leaving her alone and fearful.

She was trapped. Cornered like one of the rats inhabiting the building. Why hadn't she just run? She might be small but she was fast. She might have outdistanced her pursuer and gotten to her car safely.

Minutes dragged by into what seemed like hours. Taffy strained to hear, but no noise greeted her. Maybe he was gone. Maybe he was biding his time, waiting until she was foolish enough to feel safe and emerge from her hiding place. She took in deep draughts of air. No smoke, thank God. At least not yet. She couldn't believe eluding him was this easy. She couldn't relax. Alert, tense, she grew stiff while she waited. If only she could straighten and stretch rather than being bent and twisted like a pretzel.

An eternity passed. She even dozed off, then awoke with a start, heart pounding. She checked her watch with the flashlight. Half past twelve. Two hours in this godforsaken hole. Surely her pursuer had given up and had left by now. Only half-convinced, Taffy opened the laundry chute door a crack and listened. Quiet surrounded her. She swung the door open. Eyes adjusted to the dark, she could see well enough to know the room was empty.

She inched out of her cramped cell, each movement painful as blood began circulating normally. Biting her lip so as not to cry out, she got to her feet and cautiously stretched and exercised each limb, each muscle. She wasn't about to leave her safe haven until she was certain she could run if she had to.

She crept through the apartment to the kitchen. A stealthy check out the window revealed no waiting danger, no reason to hesitate. And yet, as she back-tracked through the opening and down the rotted stairway, her pulse raced and a rushing sound filled her ears.

The night had grown cooler, but Taffy grew warmer and sweatier with every step she took back toward her car. Only when she was inside with the doors locked did she dare to believe she was safe, at least for the moment.

But how to stay that way?

"WHAT IN THE HELL are you doing here in the middle of the night?" Paco demanded.

His features were sleep-mellowed, but that was the only soft thing about him. His tone was strident. And because he was wearing nothing but cotton pajama bottoms, Taffy had a clear view of every well-drawn, hard-looking muscle of his lightly bronzed, smooth-skinned torso. She also noticed the drawstring hung out from the waistband as if he'd hurriedly had to pull on the bottoms before answering her insistent ring.

Forcing her gaze back to his face, she said, "I'm in trouble and I didn't know where else to go."

He yawned, swiped an impatient hand across his eyes and stepped back. "C'mon in."

Though she felt bandy-legged, Taffy raced up the stairs before he could change his mind. Her stomach did a little dance waiting for him to catch up.

"Now what's this about trouble?" he asked, closing and locking the apartment door behind him.

Taffy delved right into her story faster than a loco-motive. "When I arrived home earlier this evening, I found a note in my mail saying I should meet you at this building up north, and I figured you were testing me so I went and—"

"Whoa. Wait a minute." He seemed to be instantly wide awake. "I didn't send you any note."

She took a deep breath and clasped her hands to-gether. Hard. "I know that . . . *now*."

He frowned as he gave her the once-over. "You're shaking."

"I am not."

"Mmm. Let me get you a brandy anyway." He in-dicated a couch in the living room. "Sit."

Taffy didn't argue. She couldn't fool him, and the brandy might not be a bad idea, though usually she didn't drink anything stronger than wine or a fancy mixed drink. Settling on the couch as instructed, she tried to relax. Unsuccessfully. Her whole body was protesting the treatment she'd put it through the past few hours.

In the dining room, Paco opened a section of wall unit that hid a portable bar. Pulling out a bottle and a glass, he poured as he padded back toward her, his feet as bare, if not as spectacularly impressive, as his chest.

He held out the drink. "Here. Sip on this."

Taffy took the glass from him, but even a small quantity of the stuff was repulsive. She almost choked on the liquid. She had to admit it was effective. Within seconds a steadying warmth filled her from nose to toes.

"Better?" Paco asked, sitting next to her and relaxing against the arm of the couch.

"Some."

"So you got a note that said what?"

Digging in her trouser pocket, Taffy took out the missive and handed it over, though she didn't wait until he'd finished before saying, "I followed what I thought were your instructions. I was waiting for quite a while before I began to suspect the note wasn't from you, after all."

"Did you try to call me to verify this?"

Taffy's cheeks grew warm, but she blamed her reaction on the brandy. "No." She waited for the denigrating comment she was certain would follow. When none came, pleasantly surprising her, she went on with her story. "As soon as I figured out I'd been had, I left. Only I didn't go alone."

"Someone was following you. Did you see what the person looked like?"

"Too dark. He seemed average, that's all." She took another sip of the brandy for the courage she needed to get through the rest. She didn't want to think about the agony she went through, no less talk about it, so she summed it up as neatly as possible. "I tricked him, made him think I was going into an apartment, but I gave him the slip and hid in the abandoned building next door."

"Quick thinking."

"He, uh, did search part of the building, but he d-didn't find me." Her voice quavered. She absolutely couldn't tell him where she'd been hiding or how truly terrified she had been. Sharing all of the details with a man who had no limits for himself would be too humiliating. She took another sip of the brandy, and said, "I w-waited a long time before leaving the place."

And before she knew it, she was gathered into strong arms and held fast. His voice comforting, he told her, "You're safe now."

For the moment hung between them, unspoken.

And for the moment, Taffy was thankful that she didn't have to be alone. She relaxed against Paco's chest, blamed it on the brandy. He felt so good. Leaning on him felt so right.

"I had a lot of time to think while I was holed up, waiting for the creep to get lost," she said, relaxing under the delicious stroking of his hand on her back. "It had to be the guy who set the fire, right?"

"Seems so."

"I guess he doesn't care that I can't remember what he looks like. He just wants me out of the way."

"Memories come back."

Her cheek pressed against warm, smooth skin, Taffy nodded. His response to the movement was instantaneous. He stiffened. She waited for him to push her away, but the calm stroking continued.

"And since he used your name to get me to come," she said, "chances are he knows we're working together."

Paco merely cleared his throat and murmured, "Mmm."

Taffy pushed far enough away to give him a suspicious look. "And you probably have more to do with the fire than even you know. What did you find in those pictures?"

"Nothing concrete. I thought there might be a connection with the fire, but only some of those prints were on display at Endeavors. By the time I got done replacing all the missing prints, I was too tired to make sense of anything."

"I'm not. I mean, I'm physically worn out, but I'm not sleepy."

"Does that mean you're going to keep me up all night talking?"

"That depends."

"On what?"

"On what we find in those photographs."

Taffy pushed away from him and imagined he let go of her somewhat reluctantly. But when she searched his expression, it was void of any telling emotion.

"Give me a minute to get properly dressed," he said.

As he left the room, she murmured, "I wasn't complaining."

He was in his bedroom doorway before he just as softly returned, "I heard that."

But he didn't sound disapproving. For the first time since her night of terror began, Taffy had reason to smile.

THOUGH PACO HAD OFFERED Taffy no recriminations—for what good would it have done to tell her something she already knew?—he could hardly believe she'd been foolish enough to set off for that bogus rendezvous alone. Exactly as he'd thought, she was too trusting. And so naive.

So upper-class.

With that reminder hardening him against the memory of the way she'd felt in his arms, Paco stripped off his pajama bottoms and drew on jeans and a cotton sweater as if the more substantial clothing were protective armor.

Taffy Darling was also one smart lady, he had to give her that. Not many women would have been able to think on their feet so quickly given the frightening circumstances. And Taffy had been badly frightened. He recognized this, no matter how brave she was trying to be.

He should have warned her, Paco thought guiltily, should have told her to be extra careful because he was certain the arsonist would come back for her. But he'd been too busy trying to placate her and trying to get her off his back. If anything had happened to Taffy, he would have been to blame. He hated this unwanted feeling of responsibility. Hated that Taffy had felt so good in his arms. It seemed that, no matter his own wishes, he was stuck with her, and that didn't sit well on a man who avoided entanglements with women out of his own class.

He didn't want to think about the possibility that Ramon might have been the one stalking her.

Shoving his feet into a pair of well-worn loafers, Paco left the sanctuary of his bedroom. As he approached the living room, Taffy turned toward him, her expression intent, making him feel oddly self-conscious. She seemed calmer now. The brandy had done its work.

"Ready to check out those pictures?" he asked.

"If you are."

Taffy got to her feet and followed him downstairs to his darkroom where he'd left the newly developed prints to dry on mesh racks. They gathered up the eight-by-tens and brought them out to the worktable where Paco snapped on a series of lights that brightly illuminated the entire surface.

"Let's spread out the pictures," he suggested. "Maybe looking at all of them together will make something click."

As they set out the seventeen prints in three neat rows, their hands accidentally brushed and Paco quickly covered his reaction by moving away.

"Something wrong?" she asked.

"I'm just getting a magnifying glass," he muttered, but her raised eyebrows told him she wasn't fooled.

So she must feel the chemistry, too, only it didn't seem to bother her the way it did him. But then Paco suspected Taffy went through life without limitations. He opened a desk drawer and rooted around inside for a moment before he triumphantly pulled out the magnifying glass and gave her a look that said, *See, here it is—you were wrong.*

Taffy's eyebrows only arched higher.

But her light mood quickly altered as they began inspecting the prints together.

"These were taken all over the city," he told her, pointing to the particular shots as he explained. "Housing projects on the south side. A mission in the downtown area. Drug addicts on the near west side. Prostitution and gang activity to the north." The stuff Gilbert had been interested in earlier.

"Latin Lovers," she murmured thoughtfully, as she lifted one of the prints.

"That's Ace Vigil, the leader," he said, tapping the image of the arrogant twenty-year-old who'd posed willingly for this particular shot with several of his lieutenants. Paco had taken this before Ramon had become one of the Latin Lovers.

Taffy used the magnifying glass to inspect each face carefully. She took her time, keeping Paco on edge. His heart fell when she shook her head and said, "I don't recognize any of them."

He'd been hoping she would indict one of them, thereby clearing his brother. Now it was looking even more likely that Ramon could be involved. Paco didn't fool himself—even a good kid was likely to turn fast under a bad influence. He wasn't yet willing to share his uneasy suppositions with Taffy. He wanted to question Ramon himself.

She set down the print and asked, "So which of these photographs were on display at Endeavors?"

Paco quickly reshuffled the glossies, setting the copies of the display prints in the top row, the others below. Altogether there were five photos that would have been in the show, plus twelve others.

Taffy started moving the last around until they were grouped to her satisfaction. "Five display prints and five related groups of shots."

She was correct. Although photos other than those in the show had been stolen, all the reprints had come from the same five shots.

"A pattern," he said, giving her credit yet again for seeing something he hadn't earlier. "Now the question is which of the sets should we be concentrating on?"

"The obvious answer would be the gang, but I don't recognize any of them." She glanced at the two related photographs, one focusing on a couple of guys in a mock fight, the other of several members checking weapons while preparing for a serious battle with a rival gang. "No one new here," she murmured.

"Right. Looks like this isn't going to get us anywhere, after all."

But Taffy was still concentrating, this time on the photographs of prostitutes working Latin Lovers' territory. She shuffled through all four, then backtracked.

"Wait a minute."

She stared at a long shot of a lone prostitute standing in front of a club. Paco remembered taking this from more of a distance than usual so he wouldn't be spotted and could get some unselfconscious shots. The woman was young, a teenager, and Paco remembered she'd been very, very angry, arguing with a man Paco had assumed was her pimp. He'd also figured the hassle was over money.

Taffy pulled the print closer to the lights and used the magnifying glass to get a better image. A pulse beat in her throat erratically when she said, "There's something very familiar about him."

Wearing black leather, greasy hair hanging wild over his forehead, the man in the photograph was half-turned from the camera, only his right side open to view. Paco never had gotten a decent shot of his whole face.

"Familiar how?" he asked.

"It's his stance. The way it's so threatening...like when the arsonist tried to kill me. And his clothes..." Eyes wide, her breathing shallow, Taffy faced Paco and handed over the print and magnifying glass. "Look hard at his hair and you can make out the Latin Lovers sweatband!" She shivered. "Just seeing this gives me the chills. Now if only I could actually see his whole face..."

When Paco took a better look, he had the opposite reaction. He grew warm all over—with relief! Though the guy's turned-away face was unrecognizable, he knew this wasn't Ramon.

"Here's the link," Taffy continued excitedly. "Do you realize what this means?"

"Yeah, that I have someplace to start investigating in the morning."

She frowned at him, and quickly amended, "*We* have a place. *Partners,* remember?"

"Mmm," Paco grunted, unwilling to commit himself.

Now he would not only have to think of a way to
keep Taffy busy elsewhere, he had to make certain that
"elsewhere" was safe.

Chapter Six

Taffy rubbed the chill out of her arms. She hadn't been kidding. She'd grown cold just staring at the photograph. The terror of the fire was vivid in her mind. Now if only she could see the face clearly!

Realizing Paco had never let her finish her statement about the photo being the link, she said, "You know, you're missing something here."

"What's that?" He set the photo down on the table and began gathering the others together.

"The original print of this shot burned in Endeavors, right?"

"Right."

"And this man is probably the arsonist. I'd put money on it. So why would a gang member from a mid-north area want to burn a downtown building?"

"Maybe someone paid him."

"Or maybe he was trying to destroy *this* photograph."

"But what could be so damaging?" Paco asked. He picked it up again. "What was it he didn't want anyone else to see? And how did he know it was on display at Endeavors?"

"Maybe he just walked into the place," Taffy suggested, though she wasn't so sure about that. Maybe someone else had seen it, someone who'd then told him. "And maybe this could be evidence that could convict him of some crime."

"Like what? Prostitution is illegal, but it's not exactly a big deal in this city. Though I've never heard of the Latin Lovers mixed up in the working girls' trade anyway," Paco said. "Muggings, car thefts, possibly even burglary. But not prostitution."

"Know anyone who can tell you for sure?"

"Yeah, I do."

He went back to cleaning up, and Taffy tried not to fume. He didn't want to tell her who, that was obvious, but in the end she would find out.

"So I guess there's nothing more that we can do tonight," she said.

"Just get some much-needed sleep."

Reminded of the way he had greeted her at the door, Taffy felt her cheeks warm. "I hope I can sleep." She never thought she would feel unsafe in her own apartment. "I guess I'd better get home."

"You're not going home."

"I thought we just agreed there wasn't anything else we could do until morning."

"I said sleep, and I doubt you'll do much of that if you go back to your apartment. The arsonist might be waiting for you, you know."

Taffy's stomach knotted at the very thought. "If you're trying to scare me, you're doing a swell job."

"I'm trying to be truthful, something I should have been earlier."

"You guessed he would come after me?" When Paco nodded, Taffy's fear and anger flared. "Then why didn't you say something?" she yelled. "Why didn't you warn me?"

"I should have."

His admission deflated her righteous indignation.

"But you should have thought about the possibility, too," he added.

"*I'm* not the one who associates with criminal types. I don't know how they think."

Paco set his jaw. "Then you'd better learn. Fast."

Taffy wanted to hit him, she really did. And if he didn't seem so concerned about her welfare, she might have. Instead she took a deep breath and told herself to be patient. He was, after all, the man who'd saved her life in the first place.

"So what do you suggest I do? It's too late to go to my parents' home. But I guess I could check into a hotel." Not that she had money to burn.

"You're going to stay here."

"Who says?"

"Me. And don't give me lip or I'll carry you to the spare bedroom and hog-tie you to the bed."

"Hog-tie? You've been watching too many old westerns!"

Paco took a threatening step toward her, and Taffy backed away, right into a filing cabinet. Her teeth jarred together and her aching joints protested.

"I'm not letting you out of my sight," he threatened, "at least not tonight. You need protection."

"Not out of your sight?" Taffy's pulse picked up at the images she immediately conjured—like Paco in those pajama bottoms. What was she thinking? He was too arrogant for words! Nevertheless, she heard herself asking, "What happened to the spare bedroom?"

"Okay, not out of my hearing range, then."

"All right."

"All right?"

He studied her suspiciously as if he couldn't believe she'd given in without more of a fight. Taffy told herself she did so because she was too exhausted to continue arguing and too sore to let him carry through with his silly threats. That she felt safe with him was an added bonus.

"You win this round," she told him, "as long as you let me get to your spare bedroom on my own two feet."

"Done."

A few minutes later they trudged up the stairs. As Taffy followed Paco through the dining room to the short hallway, she wondered where he'd put her present. Probably in the back of some closet. She vowed not to ask.

"You'll use this room." He opened a door and flicked on a light. "I'll get you something to sleep in. There's a terry robe in the closet. Sorry, but no private bath. You'll have to share with me," he said, indicating one of two doors on the other side of the hall.

He left her abruptly, opened the other door and slipped into his bedroom.

Taffy entered her room and was pleasantly surprised by the decor. Rather than the stark black and white of the living area, the bedroom was decked with color. Spread, pillows, rug, bedside lamp and vase on the dresser were clearly of Mexican influence. Hand-embroidered with thousands of flowers, the bed-spread especially was beautiful. And the wooden furniture was hand-carved.

"It's not classy, but you can sleep safe here." Paco was lounging in the doorway, T-shirt in hand, hooded dark eyes fixed on her.

Taffy self-consciously fingered the embroidery of the cover. "It's a very special room. And the spread..."

"My mother's a very special woman."

"She made this? It's beautiful."

He held out the thin white garment she was to wear as a nightshirt. Their fingers brushed as she took it from him, and Taffy felt the same chemistry she had earlier.

"You'll find a new toothbrush in the medicine cabinet." He backed off. "Good night."

"Night."

She found the terry robe and headed for the bathroom where she cleaned up and climbed into Paco's T-shirt. It was soft and warm against her skin, and though it was clean, she imagined she was enveloped by his comforting male scent.

Too bad she wasn't comfortable enough to sleep. Carefully she folded down the bedspread to the foot of the bed and climbed in. But every time she closed her eyes, she saw *him* looming over her.

Greasy strands of dark hair falling over his forehead... Latin Lovers sweatband... threatening body stance.

And when she heard strange noises in the darkened apartment, her heart began to race.

Suddenly the bed bounced and a solid weight landed on her chest. With a muffled squeal, Taffy whipped up only to have a cat chastise her grumpily and scamper away.

"Kitty," she whispered. "I'm sorry. Come back. I don't want to be alone." She heard the thump-thump of paws racing down the hall, a second set following.

And Taffy stared, eyes wide, into the dark. She couldn't sleep. Maybe Paco could talk her into relaxing, she thought, grabbing the robe as she slipped from the bed. When she got to his door, it was slightly ajar, probably from the cats. She peeked in but could see nothing but blurry silhouettes. A soft snore came from the other side of the room and the springs squeaked as Paco turned in his sleep.

Great. What now?

Acting on impulse, Taffy went to her room, pulled a light blanket and a pillow from her bed and quickly returned to Paco's bedroom. "Paco?" she whispered, to make certain he was still fast asleep.

His heavy breathing was her only answer.

She inched the door open, slipped inside and crossed the room on tiptoes. Letting the soft sounds he made every once in a while be her guide, she found her way to the bed. He showed no signs of awakening. With a sigh of relief, Taffy quietly sank to the floor, using her pillow and blanket as a makeshift bed. So she might not be able to sleep, but she could at least feel comforted by Paco's presence.

And at the first crack of dawn, she would return to her own bed.

Paco would never be the wiser.

HOLED UP IN HIS CAR across from the two flat, he waited for Taffy Darling to leave.

He'd been waiting far too long already and for the second time that night. When he'd lost her somewhere around the abandoned building earlier, he'd searched for her vehicle. Piece of cake. Not many red MGs in that neighborhood. His own car had been parked up the street and he'd figured it as good a place as any to settle in.

She'd taken her time showing then, and she was taking even more time now.

He watched the lights go out one by one, but still the front door did not open. The truth of the matter slapped him in the face. She wasn't coming out. He cursed whatever fate had sent Paco Jones back to the burning gallery building in time to save her. Now it looked as if the two of them were real tight. He now had double trouble on his hands.

He fingered the pack of matches in his pocket.

Tempting.

Wouldn't it be ironic if he burned them both while they were together!

Seriously considering torching the building, he counted the pluses. Middle of the night. Deserted streets. Probably no one to raise the alarm. But he wasn't prepared. Hadn't planned it out. Hadn't had the time to savor the physical thrill that always started as a tiny ember deep inside him.

And the way his luck was going, Paco Jones would probably get them both out.

Besides, he wasn't really a murderer, and he didn't have anything against Paco. Just the girl. She was the one who had seen his face. Sometimes doing an un-pleasant task was a necessary fact of life.

Doing Taffy Darling before her memory returned was one of those facts.

EARLY THE NEXT MORNING, Paco was digging under the driver's seat for an envelope containing a contract he'd forgotten he'd stuffed there, when a vehicle pulled up behind his Jeep. He glanced back to see David at the wheel of the other car.

His old friend got out and, with what looked like a forced smile, said, "Hey, Paco."

"David. What's up?"

"Thought I'd swing by, see if you wanted to go out for breakfast. I can't remember the last time we started the day together."

Neither could Paco. And though David used to drop by unannounced all the time, he hadn't done so since before the political campaign almost a year ago, Paco realized. His radar went on alert. "Not this morning, amigo. I, uh, have company."

"Oh." David's fingers stroked the hood of his car as if he had a sudden case of nerves. "Sorry. I didn't mean to intrude. I just figured we could do some catching up."

He didn't *sound* sorry, and they'd been to a soccer match together a couple of weeks before. Afterward they'd gone out for beers where all they'd done was talk. It seemed as if David wanted to "catch up" since the fire. Paco thought a one-on-one with him might not be a bad idea since he still lived and worked in the old neighborhood. And for some reason, Paco got the feeling David knew *something*.

"I've got an appointment with a potential new client this evening, but how about an early dinner, say around five?"

"Yeah, I could manage that. Lindo Yucatan?" David suggested.

The restaurant was one they used to frequent before David got so busy.

"See you there." And, as his friend turned to his car, Paco couldn't help testing him. "Hey, David, good idea of yours."

David glanced over his shoulder. "What?"

"The photo project for the newsletter."

David froze and his expression went blank. "Project?"

"I'm sure Gilbert said it was your idea."

And his eyes narrowed. "I don't know what you're talking about."

Paco couldn't tell if he did or not. "Maybe I misunderstood. We'll talk over dinner."

With that, he waved and jogged off toward the building, leaving David staring after him.

SHE COULDN'T BREATHE. A great weight pressed on her chest, making it impossible. She was being deprived of air, would surely suffocate if someone didn't help her...

Taffy woke with a start and stared into quizzical golden eyes. A black-and-white cat was perched on her chest, staring at her, its funny little face more teddy-bear-like than feline. She smiled and stroked the silky fur. Yawning, the cat shifted and settled in, effectively pinning Taffy in place with its weight.

"Uh, kitty, no offense, but you're a big one," she grunted.

The cat responded with a low, almost inaudible purr.

"I hate to disturb you, but I have to breathe. Okay?"

Rolling to her side, she tried setting the cat next to her but the animal sprang off the bed.

Bed?

Last she remembered, she'd been on the floor.

She wasn't in the bed assigned to her, either. This was Paco's room. A masculine version of the Southwestern theme surrounded her. All but for the new-age portrait staring down from the opposite wall. *Fire Goddess*. The Fiona M. piece she'd given Paco.

Her delight in his appreciation of her gift made her forget where she was for a moment until she heard a clatter coming from another room.

Paco!

She jumped out of bed before realizing she was wearing only the T-shirt. What had happened to her robe? Spying it neatly folded at the foot of the bed, she wondered if Paco had removed it or if she had. She didn't remember anything, certainly not how she'd gotten into his bed. Pulling on the robe, she sneaked across the hall. The spare bedroom was in order, the bed already made, pillow in place where it belonged. Had she gotten off the floor and climbed in next to Paco? She flushed at the thought.

Facing him was not going to be a comfortable experience.

Taffy stretched her still-tight muscles and dressed in her rose-colored trousers and jacket that needed another trip to the cleaners. Clanking sounds continued from the kitchen; she detoured straight for the bathroom.

"Good morning," Paco called.

"Morning," she said, not daring to look his way.

More uptight than she'd ever felt before, Taffy ducked into the bathroom only to come face-to-face with another cat—this one white with black patches—who was approaching a covered litter box until it spotted her. Then the cat looked around wildly, and in a panic, shot past her and out the bathroom door.

And Taffy had to laugh at the cat's comical reaction to her invasion. All the tension drained out of her. What was such a big deal, anyway? All she had done was sleep. As tricky as Paco might be when trying to avoid her help, she trusted him with her life, so could she do any less with her body?

By the time she left the bathroom, she was back on an even keel.

Working at an island stove and counter of black and white ceramic tile that matched the lower walls and floor, Paco heaped food onto oval plates. He was dressed in soft jeans that molded his thighs and butt real nice, Taffy noticed. The dark gold T-shirt showed off the breadth of his shoulders and chest and played up his dark good looks.

"Ooh, smells wonderful." As she drew closer, Taffy's stomach rumbled, reminding her it hadn't been fed since late yesterday afternoon. Still, the quantity of food he'd made was intimidating. "Are you planning on feeding an army?"

"I have to make sure there are leftovers for the other members of the household. The well-fed one is Phantom,'' he said of the mostly black cat who sat waiting in the middle of the floor, clearly looking for a treat. ''The scaredy-cat behind the shelves over there is Peaches. She won't mind if you call her Peach.''

''How about Peachie Pie?''

''More like Peach Pit,'' he joked. ''Come on you little beggars.'' Paco set down two cat dishes with a sampling of everything he'd made for breakfast. Phantom came running, and even Peach took a tentative step out from her hiding place. ''That'll keep them out of our hair for a while.''

''Gourmet cats, huh?''

''Cats with simple, down-home tastes,'' he corrected. ''Nothing fancy around here.''

''Fancier than I'd be able to do,'' she admitted. ''Can I help with something easy?''

''Sure. Take these plates over to the table while I get our coffee.''

Paco was friendlier and better tempered than she'd ever seen him, making Taffy wonder what he was thinking. But if her sleeping accommodations were on his mind, he didn't bring up the subject as he joined her and they began making quick work of the food. They talked about safe things like the weather and the Bears. Rather Taffy let Paco do all the talking about the football team. She wasn't about to tell him what she thought of the sport in general. The peace between them was too nice to trash with an argument.

It wasn't until their appetites were sated and they'd given more scraps to the cats that Taffy broached the really important subject of the day.

''So where do we start looking for our arsonist?''

"I'm going to check out some places and people in the old neighborhood." He took a sip from his coffee mug and calmly added, "Alone."

Taffy's stubborn streak immediately rose to the challenge. "We can check them out together."

"There are better things you can do with your time."

"Like what?"

"Like getting in touch with your old boss," Paco said reasonably. "Ask him about dissatisfied patrons, anyone with a grudge, that kind of thing."

"We already have the connection to the fire."

"If our theories are correct."

"Sounds like you're trying to give me the runaround." She knew exactly what he was doing—attempting to keep her out of his way. "Don't think you can keep me busy so you can go off and play macho man on your own."

From his expression, she figured she'd scored a bull's-eye.

Paco scowled at her and firmly stated, "I'm not taking you."

And Taffy scowled right back. "Then maybe I'll go on my own."

"Are you crazy?" His voice rose. "Do you know how dangerous that could be?"

"Probably not as well as you do, but I have a pretty good imagination, and after the two nights of hell I've been through, not much would surprise me."

"You'd stick out like a sore thumb in that neighborhood with your designer clothes!" he continued, plainly warming up to the argument.

"So I can change what I look like. Women do it all the time. I merely need some different clothes and some makeup, both of which I'm sure you must keep in quantity downstairs for your models."

"A few things, yeah. But you're not going to fool anyone for long."

"We don't need long," she insisted.

"And no change of clothing is going to dull that North Shore polish."

"Is that a criticism?"

"Take it however you want."

"Look, you don't want me to stick out like a sore thumb, I won't. I'm not promising anything else."

Various expressions flicked over his strong features, resignation finally settling there. "Did anyone ever tell you that you were the most exasperating—"

"No more than you are," Taffy interrupted, smiling now that she was certain of getting her own way. She finished her cup of coffee, then stood. "The sooner we get going, the better, don't you think?"

"Better?" He shook his head. "There's nothing good about your getting so directly involved. You're asking for trouble. And don't say I didn't warn you."

PACO HADN'T BEEN exaggerating when he'd claimed to have only a few items of clothing downstairs. All Taffy found in the wardrobe closet was a spandex miniskirt, a couple of crop tops and a pair of tie-up ankle boots with little witch heels. She wasn't disappointed in the makeup department, however. Hair ornaments and a few inexpensive pieces of jewelry thrown in at the bottom of the makeup case were a plus.

"While you're putting on your camouflage, I'm going to make some more prints," Paco said. "We may want to pass a few of them around."

"Good idea."

Taffy waited only until the darkroom door had closed before making a quick change. She felt next to naked in the black spandex miniskirt and crop top. And Paco thought she'd stand out in her own clothes? She'd just have to borrow a thick sweater or jacket to cover her naked stomach, not to mention to keep her warm. Luckily she'd worn panty hose under her draped trousers. Wadded up tissues in the toes of the ankle boots made up for the fact that they were a couple of sizes too large.

Sitting in front of the portable makeup mirror, Taffy decided she'd look appropriately funky or whatever adjective Paco would use to describe a woman *without* polish.

She was still burning from that barb, definitely not meant as a compliment.

Beginning her make-over, Taffy considered Paco's irritating prejudices. He really had a thing about her background. He disliked her coming from the North Shore and apparently her living in an upscale neighborhood. He sometimes seemed supportive.

In some ways, Paco thought as little of her as her family did, but why? He didn't know her well enough to peg her. Maybe he'd been burned by someone wealthy before. If so, he shouldn't be taking it out on her.

Even so, Taffy respected Paco. His work, both professional and personal, was admirable. And he was selfless, as he'd shown when he'd risked his life for hers. And yet her feelings went beyond gratitude. She was attracted to him. How could she not be? He was virile, good-looking, dynamic. Sometimes she even liked sparring with him. He made her feel so...alive!

Lining her eyes with a midnight-blue pencil, Taffy wondered if he felt the same chemistry she did. Then, again, maybe the attraction was one-sided. His good opinion was becoming more and more important an issue. She just had to change his assessment of her worth as a person.

She smacked her lips together, evening out bright red lipstick. A corkscrew hair ornament pulled her crimped hair into a ponytail off-center to frame one side of her face, and spangly plastic dangled from her ears.

Taffy stared at herself. The North Shore socialite had disappeared just in the nick of time. The darkroom door opened and Paco exited, staring at the prints in his hands.

"I have to lock up the negatives and I'm ready to go."

"Me, too."

Paco glanced up and did a double take. She could tell he was fighting letting his mouth pull into a grin.

"Except I need to borrow a sweater or something," Taffy said, self-consciously crossing her arms over her bare midriff where his gaze seemed to have settled.

He looked away and said, "I'll find you something." But she could hear choked laughter under his words.

Taffy stood frozen as he left the room. She'd thought she'd done a great job. Tears stung the back of her eyelids and she looked at herself critically in the makeup mirror and wondered why it was that, no matter how hard she tried, she couldn't seem to do anything right.

Chapter Seven

Paco found a dark green V-necked sweater for Taffy, took the large envelope holding both the copies of the print and the sweatband, and was on his way to the door when the telephone rang. He considered letting the answering machine take the call, then thought better of that plan in case it was important. He picked up the phone next to the couch only to find Luce Sandoval on the other end. Surprise visits from Gilbert and David and now a call from Luce. Very interesting.

"What's up, Alderwoman?" he asked, fully expecting her to echo Gilbert's request for the photographs taken in her ward, one of which he would be circulating as soon as he hit the old neighborhood.

"First, let me tell you how sorry I am about the fire," Luce said sincerely. "So many dreams up in smoke. How terrible for all of you."

"Thanks for your concern." Paco wondered if that was her way of leading into a discussion of the prints.

"I read about your heroic rescue. I always knew you had it in you." Luce paused for a second then said, "This may not be the best time to ask, and if so, don't hesitate to tell me ... but I was wondering if you knew another gallery owner I might contact about sponsoring my fund-raiser."

"You're not wasting any time regrouping."

"Of course not. The fire was a tragedy, but tragedies take place all the time in my own ward. I hate to admit it, Paco, but gang activity has escalated since I was elected. It's as if they're challenging me because they think I'm ineffective. I've got to do something to counter that thinking immediately."

"I can see where you'd be concerned," Paco said, absently stroking Peaches, who had jumped onto the couch arm.

"A fund-raiser is the only way I can get money quickly to implement new programs to keep kids off the streets. Well, you've heard my reasoning before."

"Give me some time." He really admired the way she'd changed from a girl who'd been only concerned about herself to a woman who devoted her life to others. "I'll ask around and find out who else might be civic-minded enough to work with you."

"I knew you would come through for me."

"Like I said before—I believe in what you're doing, Luce." Paco wanted to know what she had to say about her press assistant's visit. "By the way, I'll get those prints Gilbert asked for as soon as possible."

"Gilbert?"

"Yeah, he stopped by to see if I had copies of the ones taken in your ward." Paco was pretty well convinced the oily man had used Helen as an excuse. When his statement was greeted by Luce's silence, he said, "You knew Gilbert planned to use the photographs in the ward newsletter, right?"

"Oh, right," Luce said with an odd little laugh. "I just have so many things on my mind right now, especially the Women and Children's Protective League dance Saturday. You are coming, aren't you?"

Quick change of subject. Paco wasn't certain that she had known, after all. "I bought the tickets," he reminded her. "And the check is in the mail."

"So you're going to use them both."

He couldn't believe she hadn't gotten the message that he wasn't interested.

"Hey, Lucky, I need to use the telephone" came David's aggravated voice from the background.

"A minute!" To Paco, she said ruefully, "David's so impatient with me these days."

"Listen, Luce, someone's waiting for me, anyway, so go ahead and let your brother use the phone." Since it was only seven-thirty, he hoped she would figure he'd spent the night with a woman, not exactly an untruth.

For a moment, Paco considered mentioning his and Taffy's plans for the day, but he decided he didn't want word to get around ahead of time, especially not to her press assistant or to her brother. Gilbert had said getting the photographs from him was David's idea, and David *had* acted pretty odd the night of the fire.

"Take it easy, Luce."

He hung up and shooed Peaches off the sweater, which she'd made into a nest. Gathering it and the envelope to rejoin Taffy, he couldn't help wondering if he was holding the very photograph someone in the alderwoman's office wanted to get his hands on.

THEY DROVE NORTH in silence, tension so thick you could cut it with a knife, Paco wondering what had happened to close Taffy off like that. He was taking her with him. She'd won. What more did she want?

In truth, Paco suspected he was at fault for her bad humor. He hadn't been able to help his reaction when he'd seen her transformation, and he guessed she was ticked at him. Seeing her all decked out, looking so unlike herself, had certainly challenged his notions of her. Though she didn't quite make the grade as a tough little gang mama, she certainly was far less conspicuous than she would have been in her own overpriced outfit. Her new look was mostly covered up, anyway, drowned by the sweater he'd loaned her—for some reason giving Paco an odd measure of comfort.

As they neared their destination, Taffy was the first to break the silence. "This is only a few blocks from where I had that horrible experience last night."

"I know."

"What? You went to check out the scene of the crime yourself?"

"This is my old neighborhood." Paco did his best not to sound defensive. "And remember, I did warn you."

"You used to live here?" she asked, sounding stunned.

Tightening his jaw, Paco didn't answer. Nearing his family's home, growing tension gripped him, too.

Two flats, three flats and a few houses, all set back from the street, all worn-looking, yet most neatly kept. Neighborhood Watch signs stating, We Call The Police! were prominently displayed in most front doors or first-floor windows. Buildings where local gangs had marked their territory with spray paint had been taken care of by the residents, who had quickly painted over the graffiti again and again and again.

The people who lived on this block might be poor, but most of them were decent and honest and concerned not only about their own families but about the other residents, as well. Having organized a Neighborhood Watch group several years ago, they had managed to keep gang activity and other crime in the vicinity to a minimum.

Paco parked the car, imagining what Taffy was thinking about him now. He'd known getting involved with her would be a mistake, and he was doubly glad he hadn't done more than tuck her into his bed when he'd awakened at daybreak. He'd been tempted to do more—a lot more—especially when she'd wrapped her arms around his neck and had nuzzled his cheek while he'd made the transfer.

A woman like her sleeping on the floor—he still couldn't feature it. Something must have terrified her. Only Paco couldn't figure out her actions. He would have expected her to wake him at least.

"So this is where your parents live." Taffy sounded a little surprised but not at all critical.

"My mother, stepfather and their two children. My half sister and brother are also about half my age," he explained as they left the car and headed up the walk of an ancient beige asphalt-sided house that was two stories high, added to which was a great peaked attic. "I lived here for almost ten years. We moved in when Mama married Tito Marquez. I was barely fifteen. I stayed until I had a decent job."

"I love seeing the insides of big old Chicago homes," Taffy said. "Did you call to let your family know we were coming?"

"Mama and Tito will be gone already. They open the grocery store at eight. Ramon and Marita should still be here..." He hesitated only for a moment before adding, "And I didn't want to warn my brother."

"What do you mean, *warn?*"

They climbed the steps to the wraparound porch, and Paco knew she was staring at him curiously. "I was afraid that, if I called first, Ramon might run off and spread the word among his friends." This way, surprise was on his side, and Paco hoped he could force some usable information out of his brother.

Taffy gripped the large envelope she'd carried from the car. "Your brother has friends who are Latin Lovers?"

"Ramon is one of them." Paco rang the bell, and before she could react he said, "Let me handle this in my own way. Don't try to interfere."

"Some partner you turned out to be," she muttered.

He could feel anger radiating from Taffy, and he guessed he didn't blame her. No doubt she knew he'd only told her about Ramon because he'd had no choice.

Then the door swung open and Paco tensed for the coming encounter.

Taffy told herself she should have known better than to think Paco trusted her. She stood back, slightly behind him, and got a clear view of the good-looking teenager, who was wearing jeans, a black T-shirt and a gold crucifix earring dangling from his right ear.

Ramon was a younger version of his brother. Same
black hair and eyes and chiseled features. But where
Paco's skin was only lightly bronzed—due, no doubt,
to the Anglo influence of his father—Ramon Marquez was swarthy.

"Hey, *hermanastro,* good to see you. What's up?"
Heavy-lidded eyes settled on Taffy, and a generous
mouth pulled up into a lazy grin. "And who's the foxy
lady?"

Before Taffy could introduce herself, Paco acted
quick as lightning. He stepped through the doorway,
at the same time grabbing his younger brother by the
throat and hauling him against the vestibule wall.
Taffy's heartbeat accelerated at the unexpected display of violence.

Stretched upward on tiptoes, Ramon managed a
strangled "What's going on, Paco?"

"I want some information and I'm not in the mood
for your garbage, that's what."

"What garbage?" Though he wasn't much smaller
than his older brother, Ramon struggled ineffectually
against Paco's vicious grip. "What's your problem?"

"I warned you about joining the Latin Lovers,
didn't I, you idiot?"

"Paco," Taffy said, "wouldn't it be better—"

"And I told you to stay out of this!" Paco growled
his return but didn't even look her way. He shook his
brother by the throat, rather like a terrier with a rat in
its mouth. "Now, you going to tell me what I want to
know?"

Ramon was ineffectually trying to pry away Paco's
hand. "Yeah, sure, after you let go of me."

Paco muscled Ramon into the living room and threw him down on the couch. Without taking his eyes off his brother, he held out his hand in Taffy's direction. "Sweatband."

Taffy pulled the darned thing out of the envelope and slapped it into his palm. Hard. That got Paco's attention, but only for a second. Then he was leaning over Ramon, shoving the red material under his nose.

"This yours, big man?"

Ramon scowled up at Paco. "Where'd you get that?"

"In my office. You wouldn't know anything about how it got there, would you?"

"No."

"You're sure about that."

"Positive." Ramon dug in his jeans pocket and pulled out an identical sweatband. "Here's mine."

"You could have more than one."

"Well, I don't. Now why don't you tell me what's going on instead of treating me like some punk you don't even know?"

"*You* tell *me*," Paco said in a low, threatening voice that put a chill through Taffy. "Who'd you give my keys to?"

"No one!"

Now she knew why Paco hadn't told her—he'd thought his own brother had been involved. Sensing the depth of emotion surging between the man and teenager, she was certain the two of them loved each other fiercely, no matter their differences. It must have broken Paco's heart to think Ramon could have been involved. And while Ramon was acting cocky, she suspected he was equally hurt by his brother's attack.

"If you weren't in my place, going through my work, stealing my prints—"

"Hey, I don't steal nothing!" Ramon shouted.

"That's why you belong to a gang."

"I joined for protection. You been gone from the neighborhood too long, Paco. This is the nineties. You don't got a choice if you want to stay in one piece."

"You always have a choice."

"So you say."

"So I know. So Tito taught me. Your father's a smart man, Ramon. And so am I. We both tried to warn you, but you wouldn't listen. Don't pretend you belong to some kind of social club, because I know better."

Taffy took a deep breath and must have made some small noise, because she realized Ramon was staring at her. And seeming embarrassed. He dropped his gaze and his hands closed into fists.

"The Latin Lovers don't do half the stuff we've been blamed for. Okay, so we've done some things I'm not proud of. Small things." His head whipped up and his expression was tight and hurt, making Taffy believe him when he said, "But we didn't steal nothing from you. At least I didn't and I don't know nothing about it. We aren't responsible for a lot of hard stuff that's going down, but we're picking up the blame."

"Because you're so easily recognized," Paco stated. "Only the Latin Lovers wear the sweatband and the earring."

Taffy's gaze flicked from the now-familiar piece of cloth to the small gold crucifix dangling from Ramon's ear as he said, "There's more than one gang in the neighborhood."

"Let's get right down to it," Paco said, still towering above his brother. "I'm not here because I lost a few prints. Those I can replace. But arson is a lot more serious. And so is attempted murder."

"What are you talking about?"

"You know about the fire in the Superior Promenade building."

"Yeah, yeah, Mama told me what a big hero you were."

"This is the lady who was knocked out. The man who left her for dead was a Latin Lover."

"You know, you're really loco—"

"I saw him," Taffy interrupted. "I can't remember his face yet, but I do remember the sweatband."

Ramon was shaking his head. "I didn't have nothing to do with that fire, Paco. I swear to the Holy Mother."

"Why should I believe you?"

Catching a motion from the corner of her eyes, Taffy glanced past the two brothers to the dining room doorway where a beautiful young woman with waist-length black hair stood frozen, watching and listening.

"Get off my back, Paco," Ramon said. "You don't believe me, go ask Ace Vigil."

The young woman unfroze and stormed into the room. "What are you going to ask Ace?"

Paco frowned when he saw her. "Marita, this is none of your concern."

"Ace *is* my concern," she insisted. "He's my *novio.*"

Taffy knew enough primary Spanish to realize Marita was referring to Ace as her fiancé.

"Your what?" Paco roared. "It's not bad enough my brother joins the Latin Lovers, now my sister takes up with their leader. Marita, you find a new boyfriend. Better yet, concentrate on finishing school."

"You don't have anything to say about what I do."

"I'm your brother."

Marita moved to the back of the couch where she placed a hand on Ramon's shoulder. "You're not one of us anymore, Paco, so why don't you stop pretending you are."

Taffy could tell that Paco was cut to the quick by his sister's statement, but he covered fast.

"I'm your blood, Marita, so why don't you stop pretending you're not mine?"

"Can we call time out here?" Taffy poked Paco in the ribs and stepped in front of him before the fight got out of hand and they all said things they didn't mean. "I'm getting a headache from this shouting. Why don't we calm down and discuss this like rational human beings."

Paco appeared anything but rational. He looked as if he was about to throttle her. Taffy ignored him, pulled the print out of the envelope and addressed his siblings.

"Here's a picture we'd like the two of you to look at. This may be the man who attacked me and looted Paco's office. See, he's wearing a Latin Lovers sweatband. Either of you recognize him?"

Ramon took the photograph first. "Nah, I don't know the guy." It was difficult to tell if he was telling the truth as he passed it to Marita.

"I don't recognize *him*, no."

Taffy caught her inflection. "The girl, then?"

"Yeah, I used to know her," Marita admitted, seeming reluctant. "That's Emilia Pino. She was an old friend from grammar school."

Clearly not pleased that Taffy had taken over, Paco asked, "So where do we find her?"

Marita shrugged. "Around. She quit high school last spring and started working the streets. We lost touch. I've seen her in the neighborhood a few times since then, but not at all in at least a month."

"Working the streets for who?" Paco pressed. "Ace Vigil?"

"Ace is not a pimp!" Marita shouted.

"And the Latin Lovers have nothing to do with prostitution," Ramon quickly added. He jumped to his feet. "You got a lot of nerve coming here and stirring up trouble, Paco. Why don't you just go back to your rich Anglo friends where you belong and leave us alone!"

He pushed past Paco, giving him a shove, and when Paco seemed ready to follow, Taffy put a staying hand on his arm. She looked at him beseechingly and shook her head. Ramon was hurt, but she figured he would get over his anger unless Paco made things even worse. She was relieved when Paco relaxed and she realized she'd gotten through to him.

Marita stared at them tight-lipped, her light brown eyes filled with anger and tears. She held out the print.

"Keep it," Taffy said. "Maybe someone you know can figure out who's impersonating a Latin Lover."

"No." Paco pulled the photograph from his sister. "I don't want her involved."

"I already am," Marita stated, then with her long hair flowing around her, flounced out of the room the way she had come.

PACO SEEMED HELL-BENT on finding someone to take out his anger on, but Taffy convinced him she needed a cup of coffee before they talked to any more "suspects." If he caught her inflection on the last word, he ignored it.

They stopped at a nearby coffee shop, a little hole-in-the-wall that was packed. Luckily a couple vacated a table just as they arrived. Taffy let Paco drink his first cup of coffee in silence and let him get a head start on the second before she attacked.

"Did you have to be so rough on them?"

He scowled at her. "They need a firm hand."

"And a loving one."

"I do love them," Paco insisted. "I wouldn't have been so angry if I didn't."

"And they love you. And you hurt them. Maybe you could have been more trusting instead of accusing. Asked them for their help."

His jaw clenched and unclenched. "Maybe. I'm just so worried about those two. For years I've tried to get Mama and Tito to move to a nicer, safer neighborhood, but they won't. They don't want my money and they refuse to let a bunch of punks push them out of their home."

"You can't blame them for that," Taffy said. And the Marquez home really was a home—she'd felt it despite the turmoil. The furnishings might not be new or expensive, but the interior had been comfortable and inviting. "You lived there and you did okay, right?"

"Yeah, because of Tito. My own father was an Anglo from a nice middle-class family that didn't want anything to do with us. He married Mama anyway, right out of high school. I was six when he died in a factory accident."

"That had to have been very hard on you and your mother."

"You couldn't begin to imagine. I gave her grief for a lot of years, in trouble all the time. Then she met Tito. Even before they got hitched, Tito was all over me when I got out of line. He straightened me out, taught me what a man could be if he believed in himself. He gave me values, you know. He expected things of me."

Taffy shifted uncomfortably. Her own parents had never expected much from her, except that she marry someone they approved of who could take care of her. She only wished things had been different, that they had made her set and conquer goals. Then maybe she would have some focus to her life.

"Tito is Ramon's and Marita's father," she said. "They'll have to turn out all right, don't you think?"

"I keep hoping, but like Ramon said, this is the nineties, and it's a lot harder than it used to be for kids to stay clean these days. And Tito's not so young anymore. He can't keep up with those two like he did with me."

"So you give them guidance like Tito did for you, but learn to push in a less aggressive way."

She couldn't erase the image she had of his throwing Ramon up against the wall. He'd learned that kind of combativeness on the streets, and she couldn't imagine what his life might have been like if Tito Marquez hadn't taken him in hand.

"I've been so tied up building a business and working on my personal photography that I haven't spent as much time with my family as I should," Paco admitted. "Mama and Tito understand, but Ramon and Marita don't. You heard Ramon tell me to go back where I belong."

Taffy wondered if he even knew where he belonged anymore. Maybe that's why he lived where he did. He had a great place in a nothing neighborhood, as though he was trying to straddle two worlds. A lot of things about Paco became clearer for her, especially his cracks referring to her own background. He might have grown away from poverty, but he wasn't really comfortable with money or with the people he thought had it.

Tempted to explain that her own situation was the reverse of his, that she had gone from money to near poverty, Taffy couldn't do it. She wanted Paco's good opinion, but it would mean so much more to her if she could overcome his prejudices rather than merely enlist his sympathies.

But she wasn't the important one here.

"You know, people often say things they don't mean in the heat of anger," she said thoughtfully. "Ramon may have been challenging you, trying to get you to prove you *are* a part of that family. You still can be, you know. Money's not the obstacle."

"Money *is* an obstacle," he countered. "I want to do things for them, but Tito is a proud, hardworking man. He won't take anything from me, even though it was because of him that I got through the photography program at a junior college. The only thing he'll agree to is my contributing to Marita's and Ramon's education. Problem is, the way those two are going, they won't have the chance to get one. I'd tie them up and deliver them personally if I thought—"

"There you go, trying to use force again," Taffy interrupted.

Paco would be more than a little disappointed if Ramon and Marita refused to go along with his plans. She sensed he was already discouraged, that he already wore the stamp of defeat on his proud features. She stared deep into his fathomless black eyes and lightly covered his hand with hers as though the physical contact could help her reach him.

"You can't try to make the people you love do what you want, Paco. You have to let your brother and sister see all their options, let them know you'll support them in whatever they do, then let them choose for themselves."

"I know what they'll choose."

"Only if you don't work at making them want something more than they already know."

Paco turned the tables on her and gripped her hand. "I have such dreams for them."

Her heart beat stronger at his touch. Did he even realize he'd responded to her, reached out to her instead of trying to close her off?

"Did you ever ask Ramon and Marita if they already had dreams of their own?" When silence was his answer, Taffy said, "I didn't think so."

How different her life had been. The whole world had been open to her, but she'd wasted her education and had flitted from one unimportant interest to another. And all because she'd been rebelling, living up to her family's non-expectations. She'd had an embarrassing excess of everything until her trust fund had collapsed. She could have it all again if she was willing to ask for help, but she would never, ever consider that alternative.

Making it on her own was her dream, the first real goal she'd ever set for herself. She wanted to be a success at something that was uniquely hers—she'd even made her own opportunity until the fire had destroyed it. But even her privileged background didn't guarantee that she would have succeeded.

Taffy respected Paco all the more for having gotten where he was career-wise without monetary advantages. He'd fought hard for what he had. He was a man who appealed to her on all levels. She only wished the feeling was mutual, but how could it be when she had nothing of substance to offer him in return?

As if he scoped out her growing attraction, he dropped her hand like a hot potato and indicated her cup. "You through with that coffee?"

Taffy looked down at the contents that had grown cold and unappealing. "I'm done."

"Then let's get going."

"Where to?"

"To see Ace Vigil at the Latin Lovers' office."

"Office?"

"Yeah—the local pool hall."

Chapter Eight

Strokes was tucked directly under the elevated tracks. A train rumbled by overhead as Paco parked the Jeep a few doors down from the place.

"You're sure it's open this early?" Taffy asked. It wasn't quite ten-thirty.

"Not to the public. But Ace and his buddies hang out there."

"What about school?"

"What about it? Some of these guys quit the day they turn sixteen, old enough to give the truant officer the high sign. Others ditch."

"You think Ramon..."

"He'd better not be."

Taffy prayed not. She didn't want to see Paco's explosive temper again, at least not aimed at his brother.

"You know, you could wait in the car."

"Why? Ashamed to be seen with a rich Anglo?" she taunted him, annoyed that yet again he was trying to avoid her help. "I promise I won't embarrass you."

He scowled at her, and Taffy had the crazy desire to stroke his face and smooth away his unhappiness. But no doubt if she followed her instinct, he'd scowl even harder.

With a flip of her ponytail, she left the vehicle and headed for the pool hall. Paco caught up to her just outside of the seedy-looking entrance. He grabbed her by the arm, making the vee of the borrowed sweater spill over her bare shoulder.

"You're out of your depths here, Taffy, so let me—"

"I know, handle things. Like I said, you can't make people do what you want all the time."

Taffy pushed his hand off her arm and straightened the sweater, but the imprint of his strong fingers didn't fade, and she had the sinking feeling his indelible stamp would be on her forever.

A grimy Closed sign was tucked in the window, but the door to Strokes opened readily when Paco tried it. The place was dingy with a cracked linoleum floor and nondescript green walls whose paint was peeling close to the water-marked ceiling. A counter and a closed bar and a few straight-backed chairs surrounded a dozen pool tables, each of which had its own long, fluorescent light fixture suspended from chains.

Only one table in the far corner was lighted. Four men stood around it, two holding pool cues, the other two beers. All were dressed in basic black and all were wearing red sweatbands and crucifix earrings. And all four pairs of unfriendly eyes were fixed on the intruders.

"We're closed to customers," one of the guys said. "You can see yourself out."

"I'm not a shooter," Paco stated. "I'm here to see Ace."

One of the guys holding a pool cue squinted through the gloom. "That you, Jones?"

"You got it."

"Hey, amigo, you want more pictures of the most photogenic city leader, huh?"

Ace Vigil was a looker, all right, with curly dark brown hair and big, long-lashed brown eyes. Only the nasty scar slashed across his right cheek gave insight to what he really was. Dangerous.

Taffy could understand why Marita was so enthralled.

And why Paco was so furious about his sister's relationship with the gang leader.

"What I want is to talk," Paco said.

"So why'd you bring your old lady?"

Affronted, Taffy said, "I'm not—"

Her words were cut off by Paco's fingers digging into the flesh of her waist under the sweater.

"She came along for the ride," he said, quickly drawing her into his side.

Taffy fumed. Inwardly. She wasn't about to give him a show of temper. Not now. He'd only say he'd been right and she hadn't been able to cut it.

Instead she went one better by wiggling against Paco and breathily saying, "I go where my man goes." She laid a possessive palm on his chest and gazed up at him with wide-eyed admiration.

Paco's reaction was to stiffen and clench his jaw. His smile would have been enough to intimidate another woman. Taffy merely smiled back. And blinked vacuously. Dragging her forward with him, his grip tightening, he murmured low enough for her ears only, "This isn't a game."

And all the while, Ace was watching them closely. He was giving Taffy a more careful once-over when he said, "Jones, you're a lucky man. So what's going down?"

"You tell me. Why did one of your men break into my place?"

Ace's head snapped up and his show of affability vanished. "Hey, you loco or what?" Even as the gang leader spit his answer, his three buddies moved in closer, one putting down his beer and picking up a pool cue, holding it like a weapon.

Reaching into his pocket, Paco pulled out the sweatband. "Someone broke into my office and left this calling card." He threw the scrap of red onto the pool table that separated them from the gang members.

Ace's transformation was immediate, giving Taffy the creeps. His eyes narrowed and went flat, and his body tensed and coiled. He picked up the sweatband, and bunching it in his fist, leaned forward across the pool table.

"This means squat, Jones," Ace said. "Ramon coulda dropped it."

Staring at Ace, Taffy took in the familiar stance wrapped in black clothing... and suddenly felt light-headed. She leaned into Paco for support.

"Ramon said it's not his."

"Maybe he's mistaken."

"And whoever set the fire over at Superior Promenade was wearing one of these." Paco indicated the sweatband.

It hadn't been Ace, of course. Taffy knew that even as she looked at him. But he reminded her of her attacker, and a memory flashed right through her mind. A face eerily shadowed and distorted, tongues of dancing flame reflected over the fleeting image of strong features. An expression even harder than Ace's. Far more vicious.

And there was something else. Something she couldn't quite define that was different about her attacker.

"Taffy, are you all right?"

She blinked and the vision faded. "Yes, I'm fine." She was lying. Her heart was pounding practically out of her chest. She'd been close to seeing her attacker clearly. So close. "The fire is the main reason we're here," she boldly told Ace, ignoring Paco's tense fingers digging into her ribs. She shrugged away from Paco and the neck of the sweater fell over her arm, revealing her shoulder again.

"We didn't have anything to do with that fire," Ace told Taffy. "Did you?"

"Someone tried to make toast out of me the other night."

"That would be such a waste." He was staring at her bare shoulder.

"Wouldn't it?" Paco reeled her into his side and deliberately kissed her on the lips, his mouth lingering long enough over hers to make Taffy uncomfortable. Then he pulled a copy of the photo from the inside of his bomber jacket. "Take a good look at this and tell us who the guy is."

Ace swept his eyes over the photograph so quickly it would have been impossible for him to actually see the people in the shot. He merely shrugged.

Paco threw it onto the pool table next to the sweatband. "If you want to clear the Latin Lovers, you'd take a better look."

Ace crossed his arms over his chest and stared straight at Paco. "I don't deal with cop shops or anyone working for them. We take care of our own. You know that. It's a matter of time."

"Time you don't have."

Realizing reasoning with him wasn't getting them anywhere, Taffy decided to take a different tactic. "Are you a betting man, Ace?"

"Always."

"Then I have a proposition for you. How about you and me mixing it up in a friendly game of eight ball. I win, you talk."

"Taffy!" Paco growled, practically in her ear.

She elbowed him in the ribs, hoping to keep him from interfering. "What do you say?"

Ace laughed. "What's in it for me if I win?"

"Surely winning would be enough."

"Nah. If I win, you go out with me."

"What about Marita?" Taffy asked.

His grin faded. "Marita's a nice girl, but she don't own me. Do we got a bet or what?"

"Rack up."

Taking the sweatband and print, Paco said, "I want to talk to you." He dragged her far enough away from the Latin Lovers so they couldn't hear the conversation. "Are you crazy?"

"Not particularly," Taffy gritted out.

"What do you call it, then? Agreeing to date that slime bucket if you lose."

She didn't tell him that she'd spent most of her free time in college learning the game. "You sound like you care."

He didn't respond to that, merely set his jaw tighter and made Taffy even angrier! Either he couldn't say what was really on his mind, or he had so little faith in her that he figured she was going to get them into trouble. Either way, his attitude stank!

"Hey, if you two are busy," Ace called to them, "I can go ahead and start without you."

Taffy pulled free of Paco, saying, "We'll flip for the break."

Unluckily for her, Ace won the coin toss. He broke, the sharp sound of ball contacting ball echoing around the room. He chose stripes, then ran three balls in a row. And Taffy was starting to sweat. Paco glowered at her and gave her an *I told you so* expression. She did her best to ignore him, but she felt his eyes on her as Ace sank a fourth ball. Surely he would miss. He had to miss. All she needed was an opening.

He was lining up a difficult bank shot when she said, "Not even going to give a girl a chance, huh?"

She broke his concentration only for a second, but long enough to distract him into missing.

"Okay, smart girl," Ace said, backing away from the table. "Show us your stuff."

Taffy carefully surveyed the table. Her seven balls. His remaining three. And in their midst, the eight. She only prayed this wouldn't be one of her off days. She made the easy shots first. Three and three left. The closest ball was her five, but if she didn't hit it quite right, his eleven would end up in the corner pocket, too.

"Well, you gave me a run for my money," Ace said, clearly trying to shake her.

Taffy took a deep breath. "Don't count me out yet." Her ball rolled right into the pocket, his wavered...and clung a breath away from the opening.

"Hey, Ace, we got a ringer here," one of his men stated.

"Yeah, you been conned, man," said another.

Taffy carefully set up a bank shot. Just as she drew back her cue stick, an elevated train rumbled overhead, spoiling her concentration. The shot went wild, the cue ball dumping into a pocket.

"And maybe the lady got lucky," Ace said, practically strutting his machismo as he retrieved one of her balls from the pocket and placed it back on the table.

"Just a little rusty," she countered, glancing at Paco, who leaned against a nearby pool table. "I haven't played in more than a year." She ignored Paco's pained expression. "But it's coming back to me."

"Too bad you won't get another opening." Ace chalked the tip of his cue stick.

"Unless you crack under the pressure of possibly losing to a woman, of course," she retorted.

His buddies snickered and Ace gave them a filthy look. She could tell the taunt had affected him. He took double the time to set up his shots. Taffy's heart sank a little lower with each ball that dropped into a pocket.

When only her three balls and the eight remained on the table, he said, "It's all over now, sweetcakes. Hope you got something hot to wear on our date."

"It's not over until it's over," Taffy reminded him. "If you aim right, you'll sink the cue ball and leave the eight for me."

"Fat chance."

He didn't sink the cue ball, but he did blow the shot, and an exultant Taffy wasted no time in further banter. Ignoring everything else, she cleaned the felt of her remaining balls, then had to wedge a hip on the edge of the table to take aim at the eight.

"Ay, one foot on the floor or it don't count," Ace warned.

Barely touching her toes to the linoleum, Taffy stretched out even farther and stroked. With a loud crack, the cue ball spun the eight into oblivion.

"Lost to a woman!" one of Ace's pals said with a snort. "What are the boys gonna say?"

"Yo, Ace, maybe the lady'll give you lessons if you ask real pretty."

Face red, Ace glowered at them and threw his cue stick on the table. "Shut up or you won't be so pretty when I get through with you!"

Taffy was so relieved she felt like dancing. Even Paco was looking at her with renewed respect. "Show the man the photograph," she told him.

Paco's eyebrows shot up at her command, but he didn't argue, merely slid the print back on the pool table. "Notice the sweatband the guy's wearing."

For a second, Taffy wondered if Ace was going to welsh on the bet. Then he picked up the photograph. He shook his head, and perhaps too quickly said, "He ain't one of mine."

Taking charge once more, Paco asked, "Whose is he?"

"Don't know."

"Ever seen him before?"

Ace hesitated as if he were considering his answer. In the end, he disappointed Taffy by shrugging and throwing the print back on the pool table.

"Familiar, but I don't know from where."

And Taffy had the distinct impression he was lying.

"What about the girl?" Paco asked. "She one of yours?"

"Emilia? Nah. She's been a working girl for a while now. And don't get any ideas. We ain't into hustling customers for anyone on the street. Anyway, Emilia's a hot cookie, too popular to hang out with her old friends."

"Who are some of her new friends?" Taffy asked, determined to be included since she was the one who'd secured the opportunity to get some answers.

"I never been interested enough to find out."

"Then maybe you can tell us where to find her," Paco suggested.

"No guarantees, but try Tropicale, the salsa club over on Broadway tomorrow night. It's only open on weekends. Emilia sometimes looks for 'dates' there." His eyes connected with Taffy and she could see a challenge in them. "What about you? Sure you wouldn't want a date with someone other than Jones here?"

Paco shocked her by saying, "She's taken, so don't get any ideas, Ace, or you'll have me to deal with."

Ace laughed. "Hey, Jones, some advice."

"What kind of advice?" Paco asked, not sounding too receptive.

"Maybe you're starting outside in. Maybe you ought to be looking right into the heart of those fires," Ace said, turning his back on them. Clearly he'd said all he intended to.

And Paco steered Taffy toward the door, muttering, "You know, some women are pure loco."

She waited till they were outside before shrugging him off. "'She's taken?' What is that?" she demanded. "And what was the big idea of kissing me?"

"Something wrong with the way I kiss?"

Taffy blinked. Paco was grinning, his overly serious demeanor vanquished for the moment. "I didn't say that."

"Good."

Before she knew what was happening, he had her in his arms and was threatening to kiss her again, right there in the middle of the sidewalk for everyone to see. And Taffy didn't even care. She wanted him to. She slipped her hands up his arms and clung to his shoulders. The thought of kissing him again practically took her breath away. She'd wanted him to ever since the night he'd saved her life and had taken her home. As his lips drew ever closer, so great was her anticipation that her ears started ringing.

But just about nose to nose, he stopped moving in. His "So where'd you learn to play pool like that?" broke the momentary spell.

Aggravated and embarrassed that he'd set her up and she'd fallen right into his play, Taffy wiggled out of Paco's arms and muttered, "Recreational sports was my unofficial minor in college." She fled for the car, his laughter ringing in her ears.

And Taffy determined that she wouldn't make the mistake of providing Paco Jones with amusement at her own expense ever again!

PACO HAD WANTED TO KISS Taffy breathless, but he'd stopped himself in time. Not only was the woman a little crazy, she was big trouble—he was falling for her no matter how often he reminded himself that she was out of his league.

Where was the common sense that had gotten him so far from his beginnings when he needed it? Paco wondered as he picked a restaurant for lunch, deliberately choosing a spot across the street from Tropicale, the salsa club Ace had mentioned. He and Taffy were from two different worlds. Good thing he'd managed to remember that. He knew where he came from—as did Taffy now—no matter what his siblings thought of him. And no matter how big Taffy Darling's heart was, having her in his life just wasn't possible.

She no doubt was thinking the same thing, because she remained silent while they ate. On the off chance someone in the restaurant might recognize Emilia or the unidentified man, he showed the photograph not only to the waitress, but to the owner. No luck.

All the while, Taffy remained quietly angry and Paco regretted upsetting her. Silence stretched between them until it became more uncomfortable than peaceful, and he was glad when they were on their way to Luce Sandoval's office and had something neutral to discuss.

"We've got to make this last stop quick," he said. "I have a business meeting with a client later this afternoon."

"Good. I have things to do, too," Taffy muttered.

Figuring he wasn't going to find out what, considering her mood, Paco didn't pursue the subject.

"What do you expect to learn from the alderwoman?" Taffy asked a few minutes later.

"Luce rode into office on a campaign to beat the gangs. She should know her enemy, and she'll certainly be eager to give us whatever help she can."

"Maybe she can tell us whether or not the guy in the photo is a Latin Lover."

"Don't count on it. She doesn't know every one of her constituents by sight." Though Paco wished Luce could settle the matter. He'd like to believe Ramon had been honest if hostile. "Luce may know something about the girl."

"Ace said to look into the heart of the fires. Plural."

"Whatever that meant."

Paco had been wondering about the cryptic message. Had Ace delivered it merely to annoy him, or did the gang leader know more than he'd been willing to share?

"There were other fires that might be connected to the one at the gallery," Taffy said. "Surely you read about them the morning after Superior Promenade burned."

He ignored her tone, which still reflected her irritation with him. "No. I was so busy working, I didn't even get the chance to see a newspaper."

"The article said waxed paper was used as the fuse both in the gallery fire and in an earlier one in Uptown. There had been other recent unusual fires nearby, too."

"Hmm, that does bear further looking into."

They'd arrived at the ward office, so their speculation was cut short, but Paco couldn't stop thinking about Ace's statement that they were looking at things from the wrong direction.

What could all the fires have had in common?

THE FIRST THING that registered with Taffy about the alderwoman was that Luce Sandoval had a personal interest in Paco. Taffy was aware of the speculative and not-too-flattering looks the dark-haired woman gave her when she didn't think she was being monitored. But Taffy had to give her credit. When they'd been introduced, Luce had restrained herself from asking about the specific relationship between her and Paco.

Not that there was one, a fact of which Taffy was all too aware. She wondered exactly what Paco's relationship might be to this dark-haired beauty who was, after all, of his own class and therefore infinitely more acceptable than she.

Professionally Luce seemed eager to help them. "So many people affected by the demise of Superior Promenade. Such a tragedy. I'm especially sorry about what almost happened to you," she told Taffy. "I can't think of anything more horrible than being left to die in a fire. Trust me. Everyone in my office will be happy to cooperate in any way they can. Don't you agree, Gilbert?'' She looked across her modestly decorated office to her press assistant.

"That's what we're here for," he said, "to clean up the ward."

Gilbert Koroneos reminded Taffy of something that needed to be cleaned up himself... something a little too sleazy to allow her to be comfortable around him, though he came across as charming enough and a smile constantly hovered around his wide mouth.

Maybe the slicked-back dark hair and the thick gold chain and bracelet and the lime-green-and-orange print shirt he wore beneath the bland camel suit jacket turned her off. Or maybe it was the eyes that lacked real warmth. Something made her want to avoid him. As if he sensed that, he stared at her openly, reminding her of the way Ace had checked her over. Only more intense. As if she was fresh meat. All he had to do was smack his lips and she was out of there.

"I wouldn't be too eager to believe what Ace Vigil had to say about anything," Luce stated as she frowned down at yet another copy of the photograph that Paco had handed her. "If this guy isn't one of the Lovers, what is he doing wearing their colors?"

"Ramon says someone's trying to lay a whole lot of blame on his friends for things they didn't do," Paco explained.

Just then, Taffy noticed another man hovering outside the door. He was slight of build, and his features and hazel eyes were familiar. Looking back at Luce, Taffy figured him to be her brother David, whom Paco had mentioned.

"These gang members have no sense of decency or honor except when it comes to protecting one of their own," Gilbert was saying. He sounded righteous, as if he had personal reasons for his malice. "They would as soon lie as take a breath."

Paco countered that. "I'd rather be more open-minded and consider all the possibilities."

"Yes, of course," Luce agreed. "Gilbert will give you what information we have on the Hawks and the Kings." Concern etched her stunning features when she said, "Paco, promise me something. Use caution when dealing with the gangs. I would hate to see something happen to you."

"I can take care of myself."

"I remember."

Reading a wealth of meaning in those two words, especially in Luce's inflection, Taffy felt a peculiar ache. It seemed as if the alderwoman had been enamored for a long, long time. She tightened her jaw and searched Paco's face, but his expression gave her no clue as to how he felt in return. Behind him, however, David seemed disconcerted by the conversation.

Which part? About the gangs or the personal interest?

When he noticed her watching him, he turned away and busied himself with some papers at a nearby desk.

"One other thing." Taffy focused on their investigation. "The girl in the photo—Emilia Pino—do you know anything about her?"

Luce frowned and took another look. "No." She shook her head and met Taffy's steady gaze. "I don't recognize her. But if you leave the photograph, I can ask around."

Hearing a thump outside the door, Taffy saw David bend over to pick up a telephone directory he'd dropped.

"Seems like we'll have to take Ace's advice and look for Emilia at Tropicale this weekend," Paco was saying.

David slammed the telephone directory back on the desk before stalking off. What in the world was his problem? Taffy wondered.

"What about the charity dance?" Luce sat straighter in her seat. "I thought you were coming."

"That's Saturday," Paco said. "We'll check out the salsa club tomorrow night."

Luce turned to Taffy. "So *you're* coming to the dance with Paco?"

Pretty crafty of her, Taffy thought, feeling better now that she knew Paco wasn't hung up on the alderwoman. If he was, Luce wouldn't have to ask—*she* would be his date. About to deny knowing anything about any charity event, Taffy didn't get the opportunity.

"I'm taking Taffy, if that's all right with you, Luce," Paco said.

"Of course. You are free to bring whomever you wish."

But Taffy had the distinct feeling that Luce forced those words through her tightening lips. "I'll be looking forward to it," Taffy said, her own irritation with the man returning. "Paco and I will see you there."

Luce was sitting even straighter in her chair. "Gilbert, please show them the information we have on gang activity."

His eyes glued to Taffy, the press assistant rose. "This way."

They left Luce's office and Taffy whispered to Paco, "Nice invitation." As if he'd even asked her... or meant for her to go at all!

Just as quietly, Paco returned, "No one's forcing you to do anything."

Taffy would force *him* to make good on the offer, if for no other reason than to dazzle him and make him sorry he hadn't been more amenable in the first place. "I wouldn't think of disappointing Alderman Sandoval."

Gilbert stopped at a bank of filing cabinets in the long outer office. Opening a drawer, he pulled out two folders, one stuffed with newspaper clippings, the other with complaints by citizens who'd had altercations with gang members.

He set them down on a long worktable and placed a hand on Taffy's arm, the casual touch making her skin crawl. He smiled as if he could read her mind. "You can look at them here. I've got some business to take care of." Then he spun on his heel and headed in the same direction David had gone.

"I'll take this one," Taffy said, sitting and starting to page through the folder of newspaper clippings. "Did you notice Luce's brother was hanging around outside the door?" she whispered.

"I caught sight of David as he walked away. How long was he there?"

"Long enough to hear most of the conversation. He was acting kind of peculiar, don't you think?"

"I think the gang thing is still a bone of contention between Luce and her brother."

"You mean David doesn't want to see the problem solved?" Taffy asked, stopping to skim a recent article about the rise in gang activity.

"He doesn't think Luce ever had realistic plans when they ran against each other for this office." Paco was sorting through the contents of the other folder—complaint forms and letters to Luce. "And it looks like he was right. Luce got the public support, but she hasn't been able to come through and end gang violence or stop their criminal activities in the ward as she promised."

"According to this article," Taffy said, "the crime rate is higher than ever. Look. Here's a list of addresses of those buildings that burned over the summer months."

"This might be something to look into," Paco said, taking a blank piece of paper and copying the information.

Taffy made her own copy, as well. "I have a friend who used to work at The State of Illinois Building. I'm sure Eden could persuade one of her old colleagues to get us information from the records there."

"Investigating on my own will be faster."

Taffy didn't respond. Paco couldn't even admit she had a good idea. He really didn't think she could be of help. How was he any better than her father? She sank into silence and went back to her search through the materials, determined that she wouldn't be discouraged from making her own contribution to their investigation.

A half hour later, Taffy closed the file. "There's hardly anything here about Luce's personal involvement in her war against the gangs after her first month or so in office.''

''Maybe she's pulled back because she's been frightened by the gang members personally.''

Taffy could believe that. While she'd handled herself as well as anyone could with someone like Ace, she had recognized his potential as an enemy. She sympathized with Paco's feelings about Marita's dating the gang leader. And she could understand why Luce would be afraid to personally involve herself in pursuing him too actively.

Given all that, why did she believe Ace had been telling the truth about the guy in the print not being one of his and about Ramon's claim that the Latin Lovers were being blamed for things they weren't doing?

And how did one look into the heart of a fire?

Chapter Nine

Paco entered the trendy plant-filled, ceramic-tile-lined Lindo Yucatan so preoccupied with thoughts of Taffy that he was distracted when he greeted the owner, another acquaintance from the old neighborhood who'd made good. Approaching the fountain area where David already waited for him, he thought about how he'd pressured Taffy to spend the night with her family. After a day of working fairly smoothly as a team, they'd parted badly.

Why that ate at him, he couldn't say.

Something was eating at David, too, though he didn't share what was bothering him through the meal. The trickle of the fountain echoed over their near silence. The atmosphere was thick with unspoken questions.

"So what's this meeting you have tonight?" David finally asked, pushing away a half-filled plate.

David never wasted food, nor was he usually interested in Paco's work. "Potential clients for a good-sized job." Paco stared at his old friend, tried to read his mind. "They want a single photographer to orchestrate a whole marketing campaign from bro-

chures to newspaper and magazine advertisements.''
David was trying to look interested and failing. ''You
don't want to hear about my work. What's eating
you?''

''What's eating me?'' Anger flared through the
words. ''How about your showing up at Luce's office
with photographs you had this morning but didn't say
nothing about?''

''I hadn't planned my day this morning.'' And why
hadn't David confronted him at the office instead of
disappearing the way he had?

''Don't give me that, Paco. What's going on?''

''Why don't you tell me?'' His visit that morning
had had a purpose. What?

''I thought we were friends.''

''So did I.''

David took a new tack. ''Why are you involving
Luce in this wild chase of yours? She's got enough on
her mind.''

Was it Luce whom David was worried about, or
himself? ''Things not going well?''

''You so impressed with the blonde that you forget
your own?''

Now anger flared through Paco. ''What does Taffy
have to do with this?''

''I know who she is. I read the newspapers. She's
not for you, Paco. She only means trouble. She's
making you go against your own kind.''

''An arsonist isn't one of my own, David. Not one
of yours, either, I hope.'' That got to him. Paco saw
it in his eyes before David quickly covered.

''You making accusations?''

''You feeling guilty about something?''

David swore in Spanish and rose. His hands shook slightly as he grabbed his wallet out of his pocket, withdrew a large bill and threw it down to the table. "This was a mistake."

Paco sat there for a long time, trying to figure out what it was David had been trying to accomplish. A warning to keep his nose out of the fire investigation? He knew David too well to believe he'd threaten anyone.

At least he hoped he still did.

BARELY AN HOUR LATER, Paco had the door leading up to his apartment open before realizing someone was in his work area. A glimmer of light, probably from the studio, made the frosted glass of the door glow softly. He put his ear to the glass, and listening intently, swore he heard a muffled noise coming from somewhere within.

The door did not readily open under his hand, however. No signs of forced entry. Someone he knew then. Someone with access to the keys. He wasn't supposed to be there yet. He'd returned home early from his meeting because one of the principles involved in the new account he was trying to land hadn't shown. Had Ramon used the spare set he kept at his family's home? Though he'd been relieved by his brother's denial of involvement, part of him still doubted that Ramon had been one-hundred-percent honest with him.

Or maybe someone had broken in through the back.

He moved swiftly through the reception area and paused at the studio doorway. Nothing going on in there, but noises from beyond told him the intruder was in the office. Stealthily he crossed the studio floor, keeping to the shadows and out of direct line of sight of the office.

Just in case he needed to defend himself, Paco picked up a long lead pipe, an addition to the lighting grid attached to the high studio ceiling. Makeshift weapon in hand, he lunged into the office, and the person inside jumped and screamed in reaction.

"Aah!"

"Helen!" Tension flowing out of him, Paco could hardly believe it was his assistant.

"My God, you scared me," she said. All the blood had drained from her face and she looked ready to faint.

Remembering the odd way she'd acted the afternoon before, he demanded, "What are you doing here? I gave you the day off."

"I forgot a sweater. I stopped by to pick it up, if that's all right with you."

She indicated the black garment on the worktable, but Paco didn't remember seeing it lying around anywhere when he and Taffy checked the place over the day before. And Helen appeared ill at ease once again.

Guilty about something?

Before he could think of a deft way to find out, she picked up the sweater and swept toward the door. "I'll get out of your hair and leave you in peace," she mumbled without looking at him. "See you in the morning."

"Right."

What had she really been up to?

Paco immediately checked the darkroom. The light was on, so Helen had been inside. But to what purpose? Looking for something he'd just developed, like one of the prints that had been missing from his files?

Back out in the office, he checked the worktable where he and Taffy had left everything but the copies of the one photograph they'd taken with them. Nothing missing there, either. If the print of the prostitute and the supposed gang member was what Helen had been looking for—what was her interest in it?

At least he'd never given Helen or anyone else the combination to the safe he'd had built into the office wall, and thank God he'd secured all the negatives after he'd finished with them.

He pulled out the print he still had stashed in the inside of his bomber jacket and stared hard, willing the photograph to unlock its secrets.

NOW IT WASN'T just the woman. He paced and fumed and cursed the fates even knowing his inaction couldn't change anything. Not only was Paco after him, the bastard was trying to enlist the help of the entire ward to get him.

How had he let things get to this state?

Paco Jones and Taffy Darling. A team. He was convinced they *both* had to be stopped before it was too late, before they figured it out.

He would turn to his one equable remedy, use the one tool that never failed him. A way out was within his grasp, he thought, sliding the lighter out of his pocket.

He flicked and the fire jumped to his bidding. He stared into the mesmerizing tiny flame that could wreak such havoc but that was under his command. Such power it gave him. His breathing grew deep.

The planning.

The anticipation that never let him down.

One more torch job would do the trick.

Then he was through with taking orders from anyone.

"I'M SO GLAD you decided to come over, Taffy," Eden Payne Lovett said, hugging her friend tight. "I've been worried about you."

Standing on tiptoe, Taffy hugged the tall dark-haired woman in return before entering the Lake Shore Drive residence. Eden and Chick's apartment was located in one of the few old mansions that still remained amid the high rises facing Lake Michigan.

"And I'm glad you were home," Taffy admitted as she threw herself down onto a couch. "I needed to get away for a little while, and I can't think of anyone I'd rather spend time with."

Her former roommate and best friend, Eden was the only person who understood her.

"Chick will be sorry he missed you, but his being away on business gives us the chance to really talk. I have the feeling you've got something on your mind."

"*Some thing?* Try lots of things. I don't even know where to start. Almost dying in a fire. Being out of a job. Looking over my shoulder everywhere I go."

Falling for the wrong man, she silently added.

"How about if I open a bottle of wine and you just start," Eden said. "We've got all night."

Taffy began with the horror of the fire itself. By the time they'd finished their first glass of wine, she'd skimmed over the details of her being trapped in the abandoned building and of her and Paco's investigation.

"So the arsonist knows where you live?" Frowning, Eden refilled their glasses.

"I'm afraid so. Paco didn't want me staying in my own apartment tonight. He thought I should go to my parents' place, if you can imagine that."

"Taffy, your parents may not act the way you think of as being supportive, but they do love you."

Sipping her wine, Taffy said, "I know, but I can't handle them right now. After a long, frustrating day, I get into my apartment and check my messages. What do I get? Some real sympathy for the way I might be feeling? No. More demands from Mother to attend some stupid dinner she arranged for tomorrow night, and Father ordering me to come home immediately."

Not to mention the call from Lieutenant Sondra King. Taffy chose to ignore that message as well as the others, lest she reveal anything about her and Paco's activities. She was certain the detective wouldn't appreciate shared knowledge, but would order her to keep her nose out of the investigation, something Taffy would not agree to.

"You know," Eden said, her expression sincere, "you could move in here until the culprit is caught."

Considering Eden and Chick hadn't even been married a year, Taffy wouldn't think of such an imposition. But she wouldn't tell her friend that and take a chance on hurting her feelings. Instead she asked, "And what if he isn't ever caught? Besides, I can't hide from my problems forever, Eden. I'm not a kid anymore. I'm twenty-eight years old, and I've finally taken responsibility for my own life. I have to do this for me.''

Eden nodded. "I understand perfectly. You may be getting a late start, but you're going to be all right, Taffy, and don't let anyone tell you differently. I've known you all my life, and no one has more determination than you do when you want something."

Taffy grinned. "Yeah, I can be a real pain in the butt, can't I?"

But Eden wasn't smiling. "Listen, Taffy, your wanting to prove yourself doesn't mean you can't take some help from your friends. You don't have to do everything alone to prove a point. You didn't abandon me when I was on the run, and you can't expect me to abandon you."

It seemed a lifetime ago when Taffy had helped Eden get information that untangled a dangerous web of deceit. Eden had been on the run from a killer after witnessing a body being dumped into the Chicago River. Taffy guessed her own current circumstances weren't all that different.

"If I can help in any way," Eden was saying, "all you have to do is ask."

"Do you still have your old work contacts?"

"Of course. Change comes slow to the state." It was Eden's turn to grin. "Not every newly married woman gets to join her husband's promotions company as a partner."

Taffy was digging through her purse. "Do you think you could get me some information?" She handed Eden the slip of paper she'd made out earlier. "These are addresses of four buildings in the mid-north area that burned this summer."

"What kind of information are you looking for?"

"Anything. I have a feeling it might be important, that there might be some connection between the fires."

"Surely the authorities would already have checked this out thoroughly."

"Now, do you really think the authorities are going to tell *me* anything?"

"I see what you mean," Eden said wryly. "I'll do my best."

"Which is always spectacular," Taffy said, lifting her glass for another toast. "To friendship."

They both sipped and Taffy demanded Eden tell her about working with her husband. She sat back and listened, happy to get her mind off her troubles for a little while.

"I'm glad it's going well for you and Chick," she said when Eden finished. "Spending all that time together could be a disaster."

"We try to work independently whenever possible to keep things on an even keel, but I'm not complaining in any case," Eden said. "What about *your* job situation?"

Taffy winced. "It's hard to think about having to make a living under the circumstances, but I have to face the problem and soon. Too bad I couldn't have pulled off the opening before Superior Promenade burned to the ground. At least I would have had that to my credit."

"Maybe the gallery people would give you good recommendations anyway. They know how hard you were working and the kind of plans you were making."

"Pretty much," Taffy agreed. "I hope they'll come through. I'm not going to let certain people be right about me. My parents, I mean," she added a little too quickly.

"Only your parents?" When Taffy took another sip of wine rather than answering, Eden suggested, "This wouldn't have anything to do with Paco Jones, would it?"

"Him, too."

"Sounds like you care what he thinks."

"Sounds like I'm a fool," Taffy grumbled.

"Sounds like you're a woman who's falling in love."

"Falling into a trap, you mean. I've never known anyone quite like him before. Unfortunately I'm not the kind of woman he respects or deserves. Luce Sandoval pulled herself up from nowhere, made something of herself and works to help others." And yes, Taffy was jealous of Luce, even if Paco wasn't personally involved with her. "She's the right kind of woman for a man like him."

"You're too hard on yourself. You're loyal and trustworthy."

"So's a dog."

"And you've always been kind to people who are less fortunate than you."

"That's easy enough to do when you have money."

"But not everyone with money acts out of kindness," Eden insisted. "Start appreciating your own good qualities and other people will, too."

Taffy wondered if that would ever apply to one Paco Jones.

SHARING A COUPLE of drinks with Bill Long and other former gallery owners from Superior Promenade had mellowed Paco's mood even if it hadn't gotten him more useful information as he'd hoped. The fire and its aftermath had become his immediate life.

As had Taffy Darling. No getting away from it. He was hooked on her. She was spoiled and irritating. And smart and beguiling. He'd been worrying about her all night and had fought to keep from calling to check on her.

He was still thinking about doing so despite the late hour when his imagination played a trick on him: he thought he heard the wail of a fire engine nearby. Chills creeping up his spine, he rolled down his window to listen. His senses were immediately assaulted by the distinctive odor of something burning.

Good God, a fire in his own neighborhood! He could barely make out the gray cloud sooting the night sky. Its direction panicked him. He floored the accelerator, speeding through an intersection and a red light. Being the middle of the night, there was no traffic, no one to stop him.

This time of night, he would normally be home.

Asleep and vulnerable.

Even before rounding the last corner, he knew what he would see. Fire trucks, engines running. Hoses, water spraying. Spectators, heads craning. Just like the last time. Only this time was personal. They were there all right. In front of his own building.

Halfway down the block, he left the Jeep on the run, not bothering to cut the engine and remove the keys. No flames visible, but smoke, thick and black, billowed from the broken windows.

"That's my building!" he yelled, as a fireman blocked him from surging up the front steps.

"Anyone in there?" the man asked.

"No one. Wait. The cats."

Paco lunged for the steps, but a vise surrounded his arm. He tried to pull free. He didn't care about possessions, but he couldn't let Peaches and Phantom be trapped and not try to save them. For his effort, he found himself flattened on the ground, a heavy knee in his chest. And from that position, he only half saw the soot-covered, black-clothed body being hauled out the front door, carried by two firemen who danced around the hoses snaking into the building.

"I thought you said no one was inside."

"Let me up!" Paco shouted. "I have to see who that is!"

The fireman released him. "Stay away from the building until we're clear."

Paco heard the words as if from a distance. This was all so unreal. His building gutted. A person being strapped to a stretcher. Had Helen come back to search yet again?

"Looks like he got caught in his own fire."

"Why do you say that?" Paco demanded as he approached the ambulance. "I'm the owner."

Back turned to Paco, a paramedic answered as he hovered over the unconscious man, checking his vital signs. "One of the boys found him beneath a section of pipes hanging from the ceiling. Must of whomped him good when it came down."

"The lighting grid," Paco muttered.

"The empty chemical cans were right there in his hands," a fire fighter said.

Paco finally got close enough to see the face of the arsonist. He froze. For a moment, his heart stopped and ice filled his veins.

"Ramon."

He didn't even know he'd said the name out loud until the fireman asked, "You know him?"

"My brother."

The stretcher was lifted into the back of the ambulance. "He's unconscious, but he'll live," the paramedic predicted.

Stunned, Paco stood staring after the emergency vehicle as it shot into the night. One of his neighbors, Mrs. Conway, touched his shoulder.

"Coming home to a fire like that must be such a shock. Is there anything I can do? Someone I can call for you?"

Paco looked down into her concerned face and tried to focus on what she was saying. But before he could gather his thoughts, the fire chief took him to the side and asked him for some information. Paco answered automatically, not even able to remember the words once they were out of his mouth. He nodded when the man told him they'd want to talk to him further in the next few days.

Smoke was still billowing out of the broken windows, but fire fighters were pulling hoses from the building. The fire was out.

"Maybe you'd better see if you can salvage anything," the chief suggested, handing him a lantern with a large beam. "This place stands to be looted by morning. Be careful. I'll send one of my men with you. We'll get you more help if you want."

A nightmare. He was trapped in a waking nightmare. With visions of an unconscious Ramon filling his head, Paco entered the building. The smell permeated everything. The first floor looked to be gutted. The stairs seemed marginally intact if flooded with water.

"Stay next to the outside wall," said the fireman who accompanied him. "It'll be safer."

On automatic, Paco did what he was told, his eyes glued to the blackened interior wall as he climbed upward.

Ramon. Dear God, Ramon did this to him. To his own brother. Had he even checked to make certain the building was empty, or hadn't Ramon cared if he'd lived or died? Had that been the purpose of the fire—to kill him?

Paco steeled himself against his own emotions and against what he would find in the apartment. Destruction, yes. And probably death. His two faithful companions. A lump formed in the back of his throat as he passed through the dining room. Ruined. Everything. In the living room, too. The walls were mostly intact, black streaks running upward to meet electrical switches and receptacles.

"Peaches? Phantom?" he called.

"Don't expect them to answer," the fireman said from directly behind him. "Sorry."

Paco had to see for himself. He flashed the beam around the guest bedroom. Totaled. Then through the bathroom and kitchen. Both in slightly better shape.

"Peaches! Phantom!" he called again, swearing a slight noise came from the bedroom. "Did you hear that?"

"Yeah," the fireman said, flashing his beam through the doorway.

Paco rushed into the bedroom and heard a faint meow. He placed the sound. The closet. Opening the door wider, he swept his lantern beam over the floor. Huddled together were two black-and-white bundles, both alive, if groggy and streaked with soot. He scooped them up, wondering about the luck of their survival, when his light played over the wall opposite the bed.

Taffy's *Fire Goddess*.

Intact and unscathed, she stared down at him as if she'd protected the room and its small occupants.

For a moment, Paco stood mesmerized.

Then one of the cats coughed, and he realized they were both breathing with difficulty.

"Smoke inhalation," the fireman said, sounding as relieved as Paco was feeling. "Let's get them out of here so they can breathe some fresh air."

The cats huddled into his chest, Paco hurried, thinking about how Ramon had been with him when he'd found them as kittens. His brother had nick-named them "The Terrible Twins."

"Oh, my, are your babies all right?" asked Mrs. Conway when he swept outside.

"They will be if I get them to the emergency vet." Ramon. A vision of his brother unconscious and strapped to the stretcher filled Paco's head. He had no right to expect anything.... "But I have to go to the hospital to see to my brother."

"I'll take the cats to the emergency vet for you," Mrs. Conway volunteered. "It's all right, really. I have a car and a dog carrier big enough for the both of them. Just leave me a number where you can be reached.''

Because he didn't know what else to do, Paco agreed. He brought the cats into his neighbor's house, the first time he'd set foot into any other building than his own in the neighborhood. After getting them into the carrier, he telephoned his family, told Tito about what had happened and promised to meet them all at the hospital.

Over. It was over. The arsonist had been caught in a fire of his own making.

Still stunned, Paco carried the cats to Mrs. Conway's car and thanked the last of the firemen who were getting ready to leave.

Then he drove off into the night, wondering what he was going to tell his mother and sister and stepfather.

And wondering what he could say to his brother if Ramon should survive as predicted.

A SHRILL SOUND startled Taffy awake. Heart pounding, she sat straight up in bed and stared into the dark, disoriented. The sound clarified into the ringing of the telephone. With trepidation, wondering who could be calling in the middle of the night, she picked up the receiver.

''Who is this?'' she demanded.

''Paco.''

He sounded odd—exhausted and something more. Empty, somehow. ''What's wrong?''

''I'm downstairs.''

Here? Now? ''I'll buzz you up.''

After punching in the access code, Taffy slipped into her robe and belted it securely around her as she descended the spiral staircase. Only when she approached the front door did she realize her hair was a tangled rat's nest. She didn't want to think what her face must look like. Curling her cold toes, she stabbed at her hair with fingers still awkward with sleep, trying to loosen the knots from it, then realized she was being ridiculous.

Paco had no amorous intentions toward her, after all, so what did she care what she looked like at this time of... She flicked on the low hall light. A glance at the nearest clock told her it was after four.

He'd barely touched knuckles to the door before she threw it open and then stood there gaping at him. He looked terrible. His face was drawn and pale, his hair rained over his forehead and in every other conceivable direction, and his skin and clothing were streaked with black.

"What in the world happened to you?" she asked, falling silent when she smelled the distinctive odor clinging to his clothes. Smoke. Her stomach clenched in automatic reaction. "Not another fire. Paco?"

"Can I come in?" he asked softly.

She stepped aside and only then realized he'd rested something against the doorjamb. He lifted the canvas and carried it inside, then leaned it against the wall, face out.

"Fire Goddess?" She frowned up at him. "I don't understand."

"She protected Peaches and Phantom. I had to go back for her before something happened to her."

The truth suddenly dawned on Taffy. "Your building?" He nodded and she reacted without thinking. She put her arms around him, and was gratified when he responded and held her close. "Dear Lord, when is this going to stop?" she murmured into his chest.

"It already did."

He swayed and she steadied him, then easily propelled him into the semidark living area. She stripped off his jacket and tossed it into a chair. "Now sit." Thinking about turning on a table lamp, she pushed him down onto the couch. "I don't have any brandy, but—"

"Nothing." He gripped her wrist before she could race off. "I'm all right."

"No, you're not." He looked like hell. Worse. Like he was lost somewhere inside his head. "Tell me."

Taffy listened in horror as Paco related what happened only a few hours ago, was especially disturbed when he told her about Ramon's having been in the building.

"Is your brother...all right?" she asked carefully, afraid Ramon might not have survived. That would explain Paco's peculiar frame of mind, though she would have expected him to be raging rather than so subdued.

"Ramon was unconscious when I left the hospital." His voice was steady and barren of emotion. "Other than some scarring from minor burns, the doctors think he'll be fine."

Taffy sagged with relief and wondered why he didn't seem happier about the positive diagnosis. "Why was Ramon at your place, anyway?" Paco went all tight-lipped, and the haunted look in his eyes frightened her. A sick feeling washed through her yet again. "No. I don't believe it."

"They said the cans of chemicals were still in his hands." Paco shook his head. "I couldn't tell Mama, Marita, Tito. I couldn't."

Taffy knelt on the couch next to Paco and sat back on her heels. She stroked his cheek and felt a sensory combination of beard stubble and warmth against her palm. "I don't believe he did do it."

"But they said—"

"I don't care what they said. They're wrong. Ramon loves you, Paco. I felt it. Someone who loves you couldn't have done this. He wouldn't. Think about it." She moved in closer and cupped his shadowed face in both hands to make him look at her. "Think about it."

Though it was half-dark in the living room, she could have sworn she saw a glimmer of hope making his eyes shine as he slid an arm around her back. "Then what was he doing there?"

"What if he came to see you to give you information...or to make amends. What if he came at the wrong time and ended up being another victim?"

"My God, be right. Please be right."

In his voice she heard fear and anger and hope, and in the hand stroking her back, she felt a desperate need for reassurance. Without thinking, she gave what she could, closeness and warmth. She wrapped her arms around him, nuzzled her cheek against him. He surrounded her in return and held her as if he never intended to let her go.

His lips found hers, the contact deep yet without lust, as if he were trying to touch her very soul. The backs of her eyelids stung as Taffy kissed him in return. She didn't know why she felt like crying. Crazy.

The whole world was crazy, ready to go up in a burst of flames. She certainly was.

When he released her mouth, she was trembling with happiness and need that went beyond simple desire. "Paco—"

"Ssh, let me hold you for a minute," he whispered, tucking his head into her shoulder.

Taffy's sensitive skin reacted to the touch of his beard-stubbled cheek. She longed for a real caress. For more than that. But she didn't say anything, didn't do anything, merely cradled his head and gave him the comfort he sought. And as the minutes stretched by and his breathing deepened, she realized he'd fallen into an exhausted sleep. Wide awake now, she stared into the darkness, knowing they didn't have a future together, but refusing to give up even this small measure of closeness that she would savor always.

Her thoughts focused on the arsonist. It couldn't be Ramon. Of that she was certain. Tomorrow they had to find Emilia Pino, who could lead them to the real arsonist. Then they would trap him and make him pay.

She felt chilled to the bone.

While the arsonist was on the loose, no one was safe from his sick mind or deadly blaze.

Chapter Ten

Her fingers strangling the mug of morning coffee, Taffy said, "We have to call the authorities in on this."

Paco reacted exactly as she expected. "You want to give up now?" It was more an accusation than a question, and his features became like granite.

"I meant we can use all the help we can get—and to get help, we'll have to tell Lieutenant King what we already know."

"We don't *know* anything."

He was shutting himself off from her and she didn't appreciate it, not after the closeness they'd shared, not after waking up in his arms that morning. She only wished the intimacy could have lasted awhile longer.

Realizing her hope was futile, she insisted, "We know a lot. Whoever started the gallery fire broke into your place not once, but twice. And we know what he looks like."

"Sort of."

"Sort of is better than nothing." Taffy downed another slug of coffee for the strength to keep going.

"Last time I talked to the lieutenant, my mind was a blank, remember."

"We show them that print and you ID the guy as the arsonist, and the cops'll be picking up every Latin Lover they spot," Paco said, pacing the small kitchen aisle.

"Not if we convince Lieutenant King to keep a lid on the information. Have the cops keep their eyes open for the guy but not do anything until we're sure."

Even as she watched Paco's every move, even as she appreciated his lean, tough masculine beauty, even as she longed for some less confrontational form of communication with him, Taffy's mind was bulldozing along.

"And don't forget about Gilbert and Helen." He'd told her about his assistant's odd behavior and the fact that she was dating Gilbert who'd been interested in the photographs Paco had taken around the ward.

"I haven't figured out the connection."

"Maybe Gilbert knows something and wants to play hero."

"And Helen's helping him?"

"Why not?"

"Why not." Paco leaned on the island counter opposite her. "I don't know. Maybe. But why the police, Taffy? Why the change in attitude?"

"I had a lot of time to think after you showed up here last night," she said, remembering the hour or so it took her to fall back asleep on the couch with him. "I can take care of myself, but Ramon can't, not unconscious in that hospital bed. How do you know he didn't see the arsonist's face like I did, and that whoever left him to die won't be back to finish the job? If we get Lieutenant King to believe us, she can provide him with twenty-four-hour protection.''

Scraping his fingers through his hair, Paco appeared horrified. ''I never even thought of that.''

He looked so distraught it was all Taffy could do to refrain from going to him and putting her arms around him. He'd taken comfort from her last night, but in the light of day, who knew what he wanted? She certainly couldn't tell.

''Possibly we don't have to give Lieutenant King every detail, just enough to make her put a guard on him.''

''She has to believe us,'' Paco murmured. ''For Ramon's sake.''

LIEUTENANT SONDRA KING wasn't so easy to convince, Taffy found to her chagrin. An hour or so later, after a quick breakfast and a call to the hospital to learn that there'd been no change in Ramon's condition, they were sitting in the detective's office at a standoff.

''You've done some real creative speculating.'' Lieutenant King leaned back, her wooden chair creaking, and, using her pencil as a weapon, poked at a pad of lined paper. ''But you haven't given me any reason to believe that what you've fabricated is even close to the truth.''

''But the evidence,'' Paco said. ''The sweatband and photograph. That connects the gallery fire and what's been going on at my place.''

''Both of which tell me the Latin Lovers were involved,'' the detective pointed out.

Taffy knew Paco was holding on to his temper with difficulty when he said, "I already told you Ace denied this guy is one of them, and Ramon claimed they've been blamed for things they haven't done."

"And you want me to take the word of a gang leader and a gang member linked to a fire."

"My brother," Paco said. "He wouldn't do this."

"Like he wouldn't steal or cheat, right?"

"He may be misguided, but he's not beyond redemption!"

"Mr. Jones, it's not my job to save the souls of kids gone bad. It *is* my job to protect the citizens of this city."

Taffy jumped in. "Well, we're two of those citizens, Lieutenant. What's the real problem here? First you tried implicating me in the gallery fire, now you're ready to believe the worst about Paco's brother." Taffy's juices were flowing. "We're asking for protection for someone who for all you know was a victim like me. Are you so ticked that we did a little investigating of our own that you're ready to sacrifice a kid's life?"

Sondra King sat forward, her eyes narrowing on Taffy. "I wouldn't sacrifice anyone's life. That would not only be immoral but irresponsible of me as an officer of the law. Problem is, you haven't convinced me Ramon Marquez is in danger."

"All right." Taffy decided to take another tactic. "Think of it any way that makes you happy. Let's say Ramon is your main suspect in the latest fire and you intend to arrest him anyway. Then shouldn't you have a guard on him in case he tries to escape?"

The lieutenant clenched her jaw and stared at Taffy as if she were trying to intimidate her. But Taffy wasn't about to back down. Her gaze didn't waver.

Tapping her pencil double time, the detective finally said, "It wouldn't hurt to put a guard on Marquez until he regains consciousness and can give us *his* version of the story."

Taffy took only a breath before pressing their advantage. "Thank you. One more thing before we go."

"What's that, Miss Darling?"

She was thinking about Ace's advice. "There've been several fires in Latin Lover territory this summer, one of which was connected to the fire at Superior Promenade because of the materials used."

"What about them?"

Bingo. The detective already knew, Taffy realized. "We were thinking if you could find the connection—"

"Sorry to disappoint you, Miss Darling, but we've already checked it out." Rather than apologetic, Sondra King sounded pleased, as if she were glad she could show them up. "Other than the waxed-paper fuses in the two buildings, there was no connection. All the buildings had different owners and officers and different insurance companies. Even if the same person did set all the fires, the choices seem to have been random."

Taffy swallowed her disappointment. "I was so sure..." She stood. At least they'd accomplished something. "Well, thank you for your time, Lieutenant King."

"And the guard," Paco added.

"Until Marquez regains consciousness. Other than that, no promises." She glared from Paco to Taffy. "In the meantime, you'll both keep your noses out of this matter."

"Sorry, Lieutenant," Paco said as he got to his feet. "We can't make any promises, either, not when someone is out to get us both."

PACO THOUGHT about the detective's orders as he drove Taffy home. "Lieutenant King's right, you know—about *your* staying out of this." He immediately felt her go all stiff on him, which was no big surprise.

"Let's not go over the same old stuff about my being out of my depths. Please."

"I'm not trying to put you down because of your background, Taffy. I care about you. I don't want to see anything happen to you." He could feel her softening. "I would never forgive myself if you were hurt again."

"I, uh, care about what happens to you, too," Taffy said. "Someone's got to keep an eye on you."

Paco shook his head. She really could be impossible. Probably one of the reasons she got to him. "I had to give it a shot."

"No hard feelings." She sighed. "Going to the salsa club tonight is a long way off. I keep thinking we could be doing something positive in the meantime."

"I have some things to take care of. Like calling the client whose project I was supposed to be working on today. And rescheduling the jobs set up for next week. Then I have to check out my digs to see if anything is salvageable and call the insurance company. Whatever time I have left I'll spend at the hospital with the rest of my family."

That would be the hardest task of all, Paco decided, figuring he was going to have to explain the need for a police guard.

"Would you like me to go to the hospital with you?"

"No."

Paco felt Taffy's dejection as she retreated into silence. She'd been offering from the heart, not out of some sense of duty. "Another time." He found her hand and cradled it, showing her he hadn't meant to reject her. "They don't know what's been going on. I have to find a way to tell them."

Taffy squeezed his hand in understanding. "What about tonight? Are you sure you want to go to Tropicale to look for Emilia?"

Though he had a mind to say no, he figured she'd go alone. Then she'd get into trouble for sure. "The sooner we find Emilia, the sooner this thing will be over. I'll clean up at my family's home and pick you up about nine-thirty."

"That's silly. I mean your coming all the way downtown just to turn around and go back to the same neighborhood. I'll meet you at the house."

He could hear the determination in her tone and knew there was no arguing her out of it. "Be there at ten, then. And be careful."

"I'll clip my canister of tear gas to my key ring," she promised.

A lot of good that would do her if she found herself in a really tough spot. If anything happened to her . . .

Paco wondered what it was that made Taffy so determined and, in a sense, foolhardy. She was out to prove something to him, and she was succeeding. He no longer thought of her in the same light he had only a few days before. Maybe she still had some of the spoiled socialite in her, but she was so much more. Warm and giving and courageous. And easily hurt. Why was continuing to involve herself so damn important to her? He suspected she could hide out safely with her family until the police had the arsonist behind bars.

"Your family," he said, thinking that had to be the key. "How are they taking this situation?"

For a moment, he didn't think Taffy was going to answer. Her renewed tension was so thick he could feel it.

Then she said, "Mother's blithely holding a dinner party tonight, expecting me to be there. Father's expecting me to stay forever where someone can take care of me. And no doubt my sister Bitsy expects me to get into more trouble."

"Have you told them otherwise?"

"No. Why should I?"

"Because they're your family."

"And they always expect the worst of me. Of course, why not? I've always proved them right before. But not this time," she said fervently.

The picture suddenly became clear to him. Paco knew firsthand exactly how important a family's attitude could be when a kid was growing up. Without Tito's strong guidance, he might have traded his future for a jail cell years ago. He expected that was one advantage he had over Taffy despite her privileged background. It seemed as though her parents wanted to put her in a jail of their own making.

"Maybe you could start proving them wrong with some direct communication," Paco suggested, double-parking in front of her building. "You don't pull any punches with me. Why treat them any differently?"

"It wouldn't do any good."

"You won't know until you try."

She didn't answer, merely gathered her bag and prepared to leave the vehicle. He sensed there was something more, something she was holding back.

"See you at ten," she said.

And he would find out exactly what else was troubling her.

TAFFY, TOO, TOOK CARE of a few loose ends—returning phone calls she'd been putting off. Breaking the news to her parents that she intended neither to attend the dinner party nor to move back home had been the first step in coming to some understanding with them. Paco had been correct about the importance of clear communication. Though her mother had raved and her father had ranted at her, *she* felt better once she realized her message got through to them.

Next she called several people connected to Superior Promenade who agreed to give her references, then set up several meetings with other gallery owners for the following week. Wanting to start some serious networking as soon as possible, that gave her a sense of accomplishment. She was moving forward and *would* find a new job, if she had to wear down every pair of heels she owned pounding the pavement.

Finally she called Eden and was disappointed when she had to leave a message on her friend's phone recorder.

"If you haven't started checking out those addresses I gave you, don't bother," Taffy said. "The police already beat us to the punch. Dead end. Thanks for the offer, though."

Thinking maybe she should take a nap since she was exhausted, Taffy headed for the stairs up to her bedroom. Halfway there, her phone rang and she turned back to answer it, expecting Paco or Eden would be on the other end.

"Mr. Jones, please," came the voice of a stranger. "This is Northside Emergency Animal Hospital calling."

The cats. "Mr. Jones isn't here at the moment."

"Do you have another number where we can reach him?"

Taffy said, "I'm afraid not, but I'll be seeing him this evening. Can I give him a message?" she asked, praying both animals had survived.

"Please tell him Peaches and Phantom are fine," the man said, allowing her to breathe easily again. "Too bad you couldn't reach him. They can come home today."

Home? Paco didn't have one anymore. But she hated thinking of his pets being caged and frightened with no personal attention.

Impulsively she said, "I'll pick up the cats for him."

That would give her something to do while saving Paco some trouble. She didn't know where he planned to keep the cats or himself, for that matter. But until he sorted it all out, Peaches and Phantom could stay with her. Paco would be welcome, too, though she was reluctant to make an offer that he would most certainly reject.

Stuffing the address of the emergency vet in her purse, she first stopped at a supermarket to buy litter and food, then went to collect the cats. The bill for the overnight stay and a few tests was far greater than she had imagined, and she tried not to think about the cost as she handed over her already-burdened credit card.

But as she drove home, rather than regretting the expense—which she was certain Paco would reimburse anyway—she was thinking about the fact that he'd given the animal hospital *her* number, not that of his own family. Maybe he figured no one would be at their place, but she'd rather believe his doing so had been instinctual, because she'd come to mean more to him than an annoying appendage who'd attached herself to his investigation.

Back in her apartment a half hour later, Taffy freed the cats and set up their litter box and food. To her amusement, Phantom explored every nook and cranny, while Peaches immediately disappeared into some hiding place. And when Taffy finally settled down for that well-needed nap, the more outgoing cat joined her on the bed. Holding on to the warm little body made her long for Paco.

"If only it was this easy to get close to your master," she whispered sleepily.

In answer Phantom purred, the comforting sound mesmerizing. Paco's likeness filling her thoughts, Taffy relaxed completely and slept.

When she awoke several hours later, the apartment was dark, Phantom was still tucked into her side, and a weight on one foot told her Peaches had joined them on the bed.

"You miss him, too, huh?" she said, wiggling her toes. The scaredy-cat immediately bolted. "Aw, come on, don't run away. I was just going to get you more chow."

Taffy barely had time to put additional food down for the cats, microwave herself a frozen dinner and shower by nine o'clock. That gave her a half hour to work some magic.

Assorted garments from her wardrobe made a definite statement—footless black lace tights, a slime-green strapless minidress and a hip-length black lace overblouse. A curling iron creased her hair into dozens of corkscrew curls that she left loose around sparkly shoulder-duster earrings, and a quick, heavy-handed makeup job completed the funky look.

Taffy decided this time she would punch Paco if he so much as smiled too broadly when he saw her.

Remembering his warning to be careful, she dutifully clipped the tear-gas canister to her key ring, hoping she would be able to close her small purse with the bulky item inside. She stepped into high heels, pulled on a short magenta trapeze coat and swept out of the apartment.

"Don't wait up for me, girls," she called to the cats, feeling as excited as if she had a hot date with Paco.

The thought stuck as the elevator made its descent. She only wished she could have a hot anything going with the photographer, but she feared that was impossible. What was she going to do when this whole affair was resolved and she'd have no excuse to be up close and personal with Paco anymore? She suspected she wasn't a good enough actress to play at being his friend.

Taffy shook her head and swallowed a dose of reality. She had other things to worry about—like surviving long enough to face that crisis.

With the sobering thought uppermost in her mind, she carefully looked around when she left the apartment house and approached her MG. The night street was quiet as usual. But a prickling sensation at the back of her neck made her hurry through the pools of light shed by streetlights. Reaching the car, she climbed into the driver's seat and locked the door fast. Her hand inserting the key into the ignition trembled ever so slightly, and she called herself a fool for being spooked at nothing.

A deep breath calmed her, and she pulled the sports car away from the curb. At the corner, halfway through the turn, a set of headlights flicking on from a parked car caught her eye in the side-view mirror. Since she hadn't seen anyone else on the street, the driver must have been sitting inside. She shook away her uneasiness.

Taffy was considering what route to take when she realized the other car was pulling up directly behind her. She checked her rearview mirror. Her impression was that the car was big and old. The grill was crooked and the left headlamp bobbed slightly. And she could make out the silhouettes of a driver and several passengers.

Her pulse jumped and she made another turn, heading north. As did the other car. Coincidence. So why was her mouth going dry on her? She accelerated, whipped down LaSalle a good ten miles over the speed limit, and put some distance between her and the beater. Since the other driver seemed in no particular hurry to play bumper tag, Taffy relaxed a little.

Then a red light caught her... and a moment later, so did the other car.

It crept up behind her, headlight bobbing with threat, crouched like a beast ready to spring.

The streetlight turned green. Taffy shifted gears and accelerated, flying, changing lanes, watching her mirrors. The car kept up with her, surprisingly fast for so big and old a vehicle. But she was driving an MG and could outrun him if only she had the space.

Nearing the curve where LaSalle became North Avenue, she maneuvered into the left-turn lane, then when the other driver followed suit, she veered to the right and went straight for Lake Shore Drive, speeding through the streetlight that was yellow turning red.

It didn't help. The other car stuck to her like glue, to the outrage of drivers on Clark who honked and yelled out their windows. Edging Lincoln Park, Taffy concentrated on getting past the final intersection before the Drive. A bus was coming through, starting the turn that would bring it across her path. Laying on her horn to warn him, she rounded the bus's nose, escaping an accident by inches. Pulse racing, heart pounding, she took the final turn onto the lakeside expressway, free at last of her tail.

Watching for police cars that were often parked on the side of the road in emergency bays, she shot through the night as if the hounds of hell were after her, which indeed they were. Though a ways behind her, the bobbing light followed up the ramp and merged.

Taffy jostled lanes, but with it being Friday night, traffic was heavier than usual, and she got stuck between other vehicles, unable to make any bold move.

And all the while the distance between her and the bobbing light narrowed.

She shot along an exit ramp, tires screeching as she rounded the corner, eyes scanning the seemingly deserted street along the park ahead, looking for an escape. Another red light. She would run this one, too. Only an old woman on foot began crossing, then stopped, frozen and staring, directly in the path of her vehicle.

Taffy threw on the brakes and swerved right to avoid hitting the old woman. The little MG vaulted the curb before coming to a teeth-jolting halt.

Then the beater stopped mere yards behind.

Throwing the car in reverse, Taffy backed off the curb, not knowing where she could go with the woman still standing there, screeching her outrage, but before she could even shift again, she was surrounded.

Dark, ominous figures.

Four of them.

Taffy laid on the horn and threw the switch that activated her theft alarm. The old woman shuffled across the street as fast as her legs could carry her. There were no other cars in sight.

A face loomed toward her windshield. Evil. Laughing. A smack on the passenger side window got her attention. The thug there held a brick in his hand, and Taffy barely had time to shield her face before he smashed it through the window. The safety glass spiderwebbed into a million tiny pieces before caving in, dropping across the passenger seat and dash as if in slow motion.

Now there was nothing between her and them but the sound of her theft alarm wailing through the night.

"Too bad you couldn't keep your nose outta other people's business," the punk told her, leaning in through the gape in the door. "Now you're gonna have an unfortunate accident."

Chapter Eleven

Even reaching for the canister of tear gas on her key ring, Taffy realized it was too late to unclip and use the self-defense weapon. The punk withdrew his head to take a position at the fender. Then he and his cronies set to work. The MG began to buck and sway as the four gang members took hold of it and started rocking.

They were going to overturn the car with her inside! Taffy realized.

Mind muddled and hands shaking with fear, she threw the car into first, hit the accelerator but let up too fast on the clutch. The car shuddered and stalled.

"Damn!" she cried in frustration.

And the car kept on rocking.

The tires on the passenger side lifted from the street pavement ever so slightly.

Caught in the throes of terror, she tried again, forcing herself to be more deliberate this time. The car shot forward in first, screeching on two wheels, then righting itself. One of the hoodlums jumped on her hood, smashing into the windshield so she couldn't see where she was going. She took a good look at him, though, committing his image to memory, then turned on the wiper blades that whipped him in the face and sprayed him with windshield fluid.

"Bitch!" he screamed as he pulled away from the window and put a hand to his eyes.

Taffy swerved hard, narrowly missing an oncoming vehicle she hadn't been able to see. His body twisted and slid, but somehow he held on, his legs thrashing the air.

"Don't let go!" one of the others screamed. "Don't let her get away!"

Two of his three buddies were running alongside the car, ready to take another shot at overturning it, she was certain. The last of them must have gone back to their old beater. They would be after her all-out in a moment.

She shifted into second. Another jerk of the steering wheel and the attacker on her hood went flying, smashing into the pavement with a satisfying thud.

"I'll get you for this!" he yelled after her.

Checking her rearview mirror, Taffy saw him cradling his right arm. Hoping it was broken, she picked up speed, shut off her still-screaming alarm and took a corner down a side street. She buzzed the block, turned, then turned again a couple dozen yards down, shooting around a second corner into an alley. To be safe, she coasted to a stop in the shadow of a garage and cut her engine and lights.

A moment later, hearing a car clank by along the street she'd just left, Taffy craned to look but caught only a wobbling broad beam sweeping the pavement. Them. It had to be. Her pulse hammered in her throat until several minutes had passed without incident.

She waited several more.

Turned on the engine.

Cautiously rolled down the alley, crossed a street and took another alley.

Only when she got to a main artery did she leave her back road and head west boldly, toward the Marquez home. Even then, her gaze never stopped shifting, scanning. Her pulse never settled. She watched for the bobbing light, and it was not until she pulled up in front of the big old house that she actually acknowledged it was nowhere in sight. She had won. She had lost them. She was safe.

For the moment.

Jumping from the car, she flew along the walk and dashed up the steps. She alternately rang the bell and hammered at the glass until Paco himself opened the door.

"Taffy, what the—"

His question was cut off by her arms strangling his neck. On tiptoe, she clung to him, shuddering against his chest. He braced her with feet slightly spread, and the intimate contact made her skin tingle and her heart beat even faster. She realized she'd never felt more alive, never more in tune with the odd juxtaposition of action and reaction. For the first time in her life she recognized the thrill of danger.

"They followed me," she said, half gasping, half laughing. "They tried to turn my car over with me in it, but I got away. I lost them."

He immediately tensed. "Who?"

Her laughter died in her throat. She clung even tighter, knowing he wasn't going to like the answer.

"Latin Lovers."

SHOCK AND ANGER seared Paco as strongly as Taffy's heartbeat fluttering against his chest. Gang members had tried to hurt the woman who meant more to him than any with whom he'd ever been involved. He held her, stroked her hair and murmured reassurances until she was breathing normally.

"Are you all right?" he asked. "Not hurt, I mean."

"Just frightened out of my skull."

His arms tightened around her automatically, and she clung to him for a moment longer before releasing her stranglehold on his neck. She pulled away slightly and he let go of her to frame her face in both hands.

"If anything had happened to you..."

She smiled, the result being a crooked little grin that went straight to his heart. Paco couldn't stop himself from kissing her.

He didn't want to, didn't even try.

Her cupid's-bow lips were warm and vibrant and trembling. She tasted better than he remembered. But he'd been in shock when he'd showed at her door in the early hours of the morning, hadn't even known what he was doing then. He knew now. This time *she* was in shock, and to continue would be to take advantage.

Regretfully ending the sweet embrace, he drew Taffy inside the house but continued to keep her in the shelter of his arm as he led her to the couch and sat. She practically landed in his lap, and her coat flopped open to reveal glimpses of another outrageous outfit.

"Now, why don't you start from the beginning," he urged.

She told him every detail in a matter-of-fact fashion as if she were already removed from the circumstances... as if she were relating what happened to someone else. When she finished, his own sense of building rage frightened him.

"You're sure these were Latin Lovers gang members."

"I got a really good look at three of them and enough of the fourth to know they were all wearing the sweatbands." She was frowning, though, as if she weren't quite satisfied.

Rage muted into sadness. Paco was tired of making excuses for his brother. "They lied to us. Both Ace and Ramon."

"I'm so sorry, Paco. How is your brother?"

"He came out of the coma earlier this evening. Mama was sitting on the edge of the bed, talking to him the way she used to with all of us when we were kids. Ramon opened his eyes and smiled at her for a few seconds. Then he fell into a natural deep sleep. The doctor says that's to let his body heal. We don't know when he'll be awake long enough to tell us what happened. Could be tomorrow or the next day. If he remembers." And Paco had lots more painful questions for his little brother. "Mama and Tito are still at the hospital along with the police guard."

And Marita was probably off with Ace somewhere. She'd disappeared from the hospital when his back was turned. If he found her, he'd drag her home by her hair and lock her in her room until she got some sense about the gang leader she called *novio*.

"Paco, maybe Ramon isn't aware of everything that's going on with the gang," Taffy said. "He could have been telling you the truth as he saw it, you know. And I still believe he was a victim in that fire. What if he found out what was going on and was trying to stop it? Please, don't assume the worst of your brother because of what happened to me tonight.''

"If anything *had* happened to you..."

"You already said that part." She was smiling. Her mouth and her eyes. "Finish it."

"I would be sick inside."

"That's all?"

He couldn't tell her his heart might break. She might laugh. "And I would be furious," he said instead. "I'd want to go out and kill those bastards with my bare hands."

"You would." She looked as if she were biting back a smile.

"Something funny?"

"No. Just wonderful."

She grabbed his shirtfront and tugged. When he gave with the material, she kissed him. Slowly, deeply, sexily. Paco's arousal was immediate and uncomfortable. *His* heart was fluttering, his breathing shallow. He felt bereft when she pulled back. Her smile was dazzling and she appeared quite satisfied with herself.

"Ready to go?" she asked.

Surely she'd had enough for one night. "I am, but—"

"Don't start."

Warning glittered from her beautiful brown eyes, and Paco almost gave up before he did start. Arguing probably would do no good. Now that her fright was over, she was pumped. He had to try anyway.

"This friend of yours. Eden. Think she'd want some company?"

"Oh, you want to visit her while I go to the salsa club alone?" Taffy asked, her expression turning all innocent.

He nodded in defeat. "That's what I thought. You'd rather be in danger when you could be safe."

"I'd rather be in charge of my own life, thank you so much, rather than let some punks scare me into hiding," she amended. "Besides, if anyone presents a threat, you just give them that dangerous look you're giving me now." She tapped his nose with a brightly painted fingernail. "That'll scare the pants off them."

He glanced down at her legs, revealed to midthigh, which were intriguingly covered with black lace. Her coat was open and he continued up the green material to the low-cut neckline. She looked different, but real nice, too, especially the hair, all loose and curly around her small face. Just studying her did things to Paco he didn't want to think about at the moment.

"Hmm, doesn't look like I scared the pants off you," he said. "So how come you're exempt?"

"Because you don't intimidate me." She lifted her chin as she got off the couch.

Rising and sliding into his jacket, he fiercened his expression. "That's your mistake."

"I think not. I know your heart is bigger than your temper," she explained as they left the house.

"Maybe you bring out the best in me."

"Me and the cats. I heard how you single-handedly saved them last night."

Paco wondered what she'd been up to all day, other than getting herself into trouble. He checked out her car and realized if they left it on the street, chances were it would be gone in the morning. He traded keys with her, and while she got into the Jeep, he brought the MG around to the garage and secured it. Within five minutes, they were on the way to the dance club.

"About the cats," he said, picking up their conversation as he drove. "Peaches and Phantom dug down into the bottom of a closet and saved themselves."

"You were a real hero according to your neighbor who took them into the emergency vet for you. They could have died of smoke inhalation if you hadn't gone in the building after them. I heard all about how lucky those two felines were when I picked them up this afternoon."

"You what?"

"Well, you gave your neighbor my number, remember."

"But I didn't mean to put you out. I never thought you would go get them."

"I wanted to," Taffy assured him, placing her hand on his thigh. "Why should they be caged any longer than necessary?"

"You're the one with the big heart."

"Is that what you like about me?"

"Among other things. I want you to be careful tonight, Taffy. I don't intend to take my eyes off you."

If he thought she might take offense, she didn't. She merely moved in closer to him and squeezed his knee.

She was a dynamite woman. Irresistible. He couldn't wait till she shed the coat and he could see the whole package. His only fear was what he'd do to any other guy who showed too much appreciation.

When this was over, they might go their separate ways, Paco thought, placing his hand on top of hers.

But tonight she was his.

TROPICALE REMINDED TAFFY of a Havana nightclub, like the ones she'd seen in old movies. Large curving bar with tons of tropical plants. Bartenders, waitresses and live band all wearing colorful costumes. Tiered seating rising above the free-form dance floor. Over the years, the building had alternately been a ballroom, a disco and a concert hall. It had about come full circle and still retained the original ceiling with thousands of twinkling lights like stars, as well as a Moorish influence in decor. But, in addition to the real thing, Taffy spotted several neon palm trees and pink flamingos.

Paco took her coat and eyed her appreciatively as he handed their wraps to the coat-check girl. Taffy admired his terrific body accentuated by a dark blue silk shirt and even darker silk-blend pleated trousers. Thinking about getting closer to that body for a few minutes, she smiled and began swaying to the irresistible Latin beat throbbing throughout the club.

"Let's dance."

"We're here to get information."

"Loosen up. We might have a long wait." She lowered her voice. "Besides, you don't want to stick out like a cop or something."

"If anyone sticks out it'll be you with all that blond hair."

Taffy had spotted a few other Anglos, and none of them particularly stood out from the rest of the clientele. "If you're worried, you could put a paper bag over my head," she quipped.

Paco merely grumbled, "Let's dance."

Once in his arms, the horror of what had happened to her earlier seemed like a bad dream. A nightmare. Even as she told herself to put away the images, something nagged at her, something just out of reach. Since that something threatened to distract her from enjoying herself for the next few minutes—perhaps the only time she would ever get to dance with Paco—she determined to stop trying.

Eventually it would come to her.

Paco whipped her around in a tight circle, with each step sexily inserting his knee between hers.

"I like the way you lead," she murmured breathlessly as her thighs tingled from the contact.

"I like the way you follow. You should try it more often."

Knowing he meant follow his instructions, she grinned. "But then you would know what to expect and I would bore you to death."

He arched her backward and held her suspended precariously, her hair brushing the floor below.

"Bored? That'll never happen."

Then he whirled her up into his arms and off her feet.

"I don't intend to let it," she said.

Taffy gripped his silk-clad shoulders and slid inch by inch down his body until she was on fire. And unless he was something less than human, he had to feel the flames sparking between them.

She thought he was going to kiss her then, right in the middle of the dance floor. Red lights strobed over his features, so serious and yet so sexy. His face inched closer, and she thought she would stop breathing. She wanted him more than anything in her life.

They were here to find someone, she reminded herself, not to play games with each other, no matter how exciting.

But the excitement couldn't last. His lips inches from hers, the band finished the piece with a flourish and Paco twirled her across the dance floor one last time. Standing still in each other's arms, they were both breathing unnaturally, and Taffy knew he'd been as affected by the dance as she. Only he seemed better able to control what he was feeling. He was the one who broke the final clinch.

"Let's sit at the bar," he suggested, seeming to have shaken off the sexual tension that still burned her. "It'll be easier to talk to people if we mingle than if we're stuck at a table." Paco held out the single empty stool. She sat and he leaned in close. "I'll have a margarita on the rocks with salt," he told the bartender. "What about you?"

"How about a piña colada, light on the rum."

"Coming up," the bartender said.

To get her mind off her attraction and back onto their purpose for being there, Taffy took a good look around while Paco paid for the drinks. When he handed her the piña colada, she said, "I don't see anyone who even resembles Emilia."

"Me, neither. We'll have to ask around."

"Without showing the photograph," Taffy suggested. "That would raise suspicions, for sure."

"Depending on how well she's known here. The photo may be the only way."

But Taffy didn't think so.

Sipping at her drink, she scanned the room again. Mostly couples, but women stood alone here and there, a few eyeing the male clientele with an interest that went deeper than a dance and a drink. She passed over two of them, but when she got to the third, an innocent-looking yet hard-edged beauty dressed in a skimpy gold sequined dress, something clicked. This one was young, way too young for a club like this. Probably had fake ID as Emilia would need.

With practiced precision, she tossed her long dark hair at a man and gave him a definite invitation. He seemed interested until his girlfriend joined him. No doubt about it, Taffy thought. The one in gold sequins was definitely a working girl.

She put her drink down on the bar and moved closer to Paco so they wouldn't be overheard. "We ought to split up for a while."

"I told you I'm not letting you out of my sight."

"But you'd have more luck talking to the bartender or other customers without me around," Taffy insisted. "Pretend you're looking for a hot date."

"And you'll pretend you are one?"

"If necessary."

"The hell you will."

She was flattered by the threat in his tone. "All right, if it'll make you happy, I'll concentrate on the women."

"The working girls? They're not going to open up to some strange blond Anglo."

"All depends on my approach."

"You're going to pay them to talk."

"You do have a hang-up about money, don't you?"

Someday they would have to discuss that issue, and she would have to tell him the truth about her circumstances. But not now. She spotted the girl moving toward the back of the club where the rest rooms were located. She jumped off the stool.

"Keep it warm for me, would you? I have to powder my nose."

"I'll go with you."

"Don't be ridiculous." Placing her palm on his chest, she pushed hard. He sat. "You can't go inside and hold my hand. Use the time to good advantage. I'll be right back."

Before he could stop her, she melded into the crowd, glancing over her shoulder only once to see him staring after her. His jaw was clenched. That made her smile.

The rest room was crowded and noisy, but larger than most. Two rooms, the first of which was a place to primp. The girl in gold had, for the moment, disappeared. Taffy walked into the inner room, and surreptitiously checking under the stall doors, spotted a gold pair of pumps with the highest heels Taffy had ever seen.

Waiting until the girl came out of her stall, washed her hands and moved to the first room where two women vacated plush low stools in front of the room-length mirror, Taffy followed. She sat next to the girl and fiddled with her corkscrew curls, combing her nails through them so they wouldn't go too straight. She opened her tiny bag whose strap was slung over her chest, and the first thing she saw was the canister of tear gas.

"How are you doing tonight?" Taffy asked, pulling a lipstick from underneath it.

The girl glanced at her via the mirror. "Do I know you?"

"Mmm. No. Name's Taffy." In an attempt to gain the girl's confidence, she asked, "Am I being too friendly again? My, uh, boyfriend says I should save that for the customers."

The girl's eyebrows shot up and she gave her a direct once-over. "You a waitress?"

"Not exactly, though I am in a service profession." Taffy laughed as if she'd made a great joke.

"I'm Chica." Her smile was rueful as if the joke were on her. She pulled a brush out of her purse and began working on her long straight hair with such vigor it grew full with static electricity. "You're new here, right?"

"I haven't dropped in before, though I've been meaning to." Taffy applied an extra thick coat of lipstick to her mouth. "An acquaintance told me about the place awhile back." She figured "acquaintance" was safer than "friend," just in case Chica asked too many questions she couldn't answer. "Maybe you know her, Emilia Pino."

"Yeah, I know Emilia."

"She told me this place is a sure thing when you need a date," Taffy said, keeping to double meanings rather than being more direct. A woman who was straightening her dress in back of them seemed awfully interested in their conversation.

"No lie."

"So she must have left with hers already, right?" Taffy asked, relieved when the curious woman left the rest room. "I've been looking for Emilia since I got here, but no luck."

"She hasn't been around for a while," Chica said, reapplying her own lipstick. "Not in weeks."

"She hasn't? I thought she really worked the place steadily."

"She used to. I guess she found a better place."

"Hmm. I hope nothing's wrong." Taffy pulled a face and got even more inventive. "I had a special invitation for her, too. An exclusive party that I'm sure she wouldn't want to miss. You wouldn't know where else I might find her?"

"Her place. The S.R.O."

Taffy thought for a moment and realized Chica meant a single-room-occupancy hotel. She'd read about most of them closing, throwing thousands of people onto the street. How sad! A teenager working as a prostitute and living in a dump.

When she realized Chica was staring at her, Taffy smoothed out her frown. "The S.R.O.—it's somewhere around here?"

"About three blocks south." Chica repacked her purse and started back for the club. "It's called the Broadrose."

"Maybe I'll check it out tomorrow. Thanks, Chica."

"See you around."

Taffy waited until the girl was out the door before following. She had what she wanted and wouldn't take the chance of tipping off Chica. She chuckled to herself as she thought about approaching Paco like a stranger and asking him if he wanted a hot date.

Out in the hall where people milled around talking or smoking, she spotted him, back to her, at the other end. Ticked, Taffy stopped dead. He couldn't even let her go to the rest room alone! He was scanning the club, obviously still looking for Emilia Pino. Wasn't he going to be surprised when she told him where they could find her?

But Taffy herself was surprised when a steel band circled her waist. Someone who thought she was one of the working girls? About to dissuade the man nicely, she didn't get a chance. A hand clamped over her mouth.

That's when she knew she was in trouble.

Her screams for Paco to help her were muffled as she was lifted back toward an emergency exit. She couldn't believe it—people all around them and no one paying any attention to what was happening right under their noses. One woman saw, but she merely averted her head as she continued into the rest room, clearly uninterested in getting involved in something unpleasant!

As the rear door clicked open, Taffy got a hunk of the guy's hand between her teeth. She bit down hard. His hand whipped away, but her hoarse screech faded to nothing as he clenched her waist tighter, which pushed the air out of her lungs. Both his curse and her aborted shout for help were drowned out by the loud pulse of music.

The man covered her mouth again and tried to drag her outside. She caught onto the doorjamb and held on for dear life. She could only imagine what would happen to her if he succeeded in getting her alone. Over and over, she kicked back, hoping to catch his legs with her spiked heels. Every time her feet found thin air.

"Shut up and stop struggling if you know what's good for you," the man growled. He popped loose her grip on the frame and forced her out onto a metal landing above the alley. She thought this was it—and was taken aback when he merely held on to her firmly and said, "Ace Vigil wants to talk to you."

Chapter Twelve

Though he figured it was a waste of time, Paco continued scanning the club. He'd asked the bartender and one of the bouncers about Emilia, but while they knew who she was, neither remembered having seen her the past several weekends. And even while he'd asked around, he'd kept an eye on the hallway leading to the rest rooms. Certain Taffy hadn't come out, he was wondering what was taking her so long.

Instinct and a low scuffling noise made him turn just as a flash of green material and black lace caught his eye.

Some creep was forcing Taffy out the emergency exit!

Paco moved fast, shoving a couple of guys and a woman out of his way.

Paco was already bursting through the rear door. A man dressed in black was dragging Taffy down to the alley and was having a difficult time keeping his hands on her.

"Let go of me!" She struggled like a wildcat, but he had the advantage of size and position.

"If you don't shut up—"

"You'll what?" Paco shouted, flying down the metal steps.

Taffy's abductor swore in Spanish and turned on Paco, who saw the Latin Lovers sweatband and crucifix earring as he went flying forward. Three bodies crashed together, Taffy in the middle. She yelled loudly, then, when Paco managed to wrest her free, went flying and crashed back into the metal waste-disposal units.

The two men separated and circled each other warily. As much as he wanted to satisfy himself that Taffy was all right, Paco dared not take his eyes off his adversary.

He called out, "Are you alive?"

"Still in one piece," she assured him as the other man made his move.

Paco was ready for a sudden attack and stepped aside as the gang member lunged. The other man was faster than Paco realized. He spun around and kicked out, clipping Paco in the side before he could dodge out of the way.

Pain shooting through him, he stumbled, but when the thug came back for a second shot at him, Paco caught his leg and twisted, bringing him down to one knee with a scream. Paco wasted no time before pressing his advantage. The gang member reacted equally quickly, going for Paco's knees. They went down together, both rolling along the alley pavement. They were pummeling. Punching. Struggling for superiority. Neither able to get the upper hand.

Barely holding his own, Paco glanced over his opponent's shoulder to see Taffy searching the ground wildly. For some kind of weapon?

Finding his second wind, he grabbed the thug by the throat and shoved him away. Though Taffy's abductor went sprawling, he had the upper hand—because, suddenly, he was holding a knife. Paco could tell he knew how to use it. He tensed, was ready for the bastard, but before either man could make a move, Paco realized Taffy was moving in, arm outstretched, her own brand of weapon in hand.

"No, don't!" Paco shouted just as she activated the canister of tear gas.

He closed his eyes and snapped his head away, but not fast enough to avoid the stuff completely. He sputtered and rolled away from her. Having taken the brunt of the chemical, the other man let go of the knife, which clanked to the pavement, and began choking and cursing in Spanish.

"Paco, did I get you, too?" Taffy asked, dancing around him and kicking away the knife before trying to help him up.

"Oh, yeah," he gasped, looking up at her through a flood of tears.

He vaguely saw the gang member stumble to his feet, hands covering his face. He weaved away, blindly heading toward the street, knocking into the side of the building, then using it as a guide.

Paco rose unsteadily and started after him. Taffy grabbed his shirtsleeve.

"Let him go."

His vision already clearing a little, Paco was torn. He could easily catch up to the guy who'd been temporarily blinded by the chemical. But that would mean leaving Taffy alone. And who knew what dangers she would face. No doubt other Latin Lovers lurked nearby. And what good would it do him to snag one? If he took the trouble to turn the gang member over to the police, the guy would probably be back on the street in the morning, anyway.

He relaxed. "I'm not going anywhere." Then he wiped his watery eyes with his silk shirtsleeve.

"I did it!" Taffy cried, practically jumping. "I got rid of him!"

"And almost blinded me in the process."

"No one's going to be blinded by the stuff—not for long anyway. I panicked and forgot I had the tear gas with me, or I would have used it sooner."

"My heroine," he said dryly.

"No need to be sarcastic just because you got a little fallout."

The more fearless she sounded and the more elated, the more Paco's mood darkened. He hadn't gotten into this kind of a scrap for years. He'd had enough of violence in his life. She'd certainly had her share lately. And now she sounded as if she were enjoying the experience.

"Come on," she urged. "Let's go back inside, collect our coats and leave."

"But we didn't get what we came for."

"Speak for yourself," she said, her grin triumphant. "Tonight's my night!"

THOUGH SHE'D DRIVEN by them countless times, Taffy wasn't prepared for what an S.R.O. looked like inside. Her imagination was vivid, but it hadn't prepared her for The Broadrose. The lobby was dark and dank. No hiding the filth in the corners or the faint smell that permeated the room, a combination of mustiness and unwashed bodies. And as they walked up to the desk, the night clerk smashed a book onto the counter, making her jump. When he removed the tome, what was left of a four-inch-long cockroach lay flattened on the wooden surface.

Gulping, Taffy pinned her gaze on the night clerk, a thin man with even thinner brown hair. He smiled, showing teeth coated with a disgusting green stain.

"Looking for a room?"

"Looking for a friend," she said. "Emilia Pino."

"Lotsa luck. So am I."

"You mean she isn't here tonight?" Paco asked.

"I mean she ain't been around for a while so's I could tell. You find her, you remind her that she owes me two weeks back rent. Either I get my money soon or her stuff gets pitched out for the scavengers."

Taffy decided she'd better get creative again. "If you're gonna do that," she said, widening her eyes and playing dumb, "can I at least go to her room and get the necklace she borrowed from me?"

"You ain't goin' up there at all."

"But if you're gonna get rid of everything—"

"Look, I never even seen you before."

"We're all good friends, all three of us." Taffy batted her eyelashes at the clerk and felt Paco stiffen next to her. She surreptitiously hooked her spiked heel on his toe to warn him to keep cool. "We, uh, socialize over at Tropicale and then at his place every coupla weekends, if you get my drift."

The clerk gave her a knowing look, narrowed his eyes cunningly and turned them to Paco. "You want in, you pay for the privilege. You shouldn't mind since you're such good friends with Emilia and all."

"How much?" Paco asked.

"Let's see now." The clerk smiled, showing off his green teeth. "Emilia owes me two weeks' rent . . . plus tenants are supposed to pay for the following week in advance. . . ."

Paco pulled out his wallet and gave the man what he demanded, but Taffy was certain that when Emilia did show, she would just have to pay again.

The ride up to the third floor was in a small enough elevator to make anyone claustrophobic. It settled with a jerk and when they exited, they had to step up several inches because the car floor didn't meet the landing.

The hall was as depressing as the lobby. But Emilia's room was quite a surprise, the improvement Taffy imagined she had effected for herself.

The walls were painted in a cheerful butter yellow, and a flower-bordered beige area rug covered most of the graying maroon wall-to-wall carpeting provided by the management. The bedspread was plush, and resting against the pillows were several stuffed animals that reminded Taffy of how young Emilia really was. Pretty curtains decorated the windows, scenic posters of exotic locales and a picture of the Virgin Mary the walls.

Potions and paints on the dresser were neatly arranged, if dusty. Paco swiped a finger across the wooden surface and held it out. "She hasn't been in this room for a while, that's for certain."

"I wonder what's going on, why no one's seen her lately." Hoping for the best, Taffy said, "Maybe she found a way out of here."

Paco slid open a drawer filled with filmy under-things. "If so, she packed light."

"It's so sad. A young girl like her doing what she does to make money, living in a hole like this, yet try-ing to make it nice. Why?"

"This could be an improvement over her home life," Paco said frankly. "Not everyone grows up even with the basic necessities or with parents who give a damn."

"Sad," she echoed, reluctant to invade the girl's privacy further but knowing they had to if they had any hope of finding her.

Foreign emotions filled her, made her throat tighten, and Taffy didn't know why. She didn't know Emilia Pino, a statistic, a poor kid who got lost in the shuffle.

"I'll go through the dresser and chest," Paco said, throwing his jacket on a chair. "You take the closet."

Taffy did likewise. "What are we looking for?"

"This was your show. You tell me."

"Another photograph. A name. I don't know. Anything that'll help us find her."

Taffy really didn't know where to start.

Someone being forced to these circumstances was way past her experience. But not Paco's. He'd cer-tainly warned her. No wonder he'd been so antago-nistic toward her at first. He'd been resentful of her easy background and couldn't possibly have known how unhappy that very environment had made her.

Then, again, in comparison to Emilia, what did she have to complain about?

Taffy started on the closet, immediately noting most of the garments were "work" clothes. Spangly and skimpy.

She'd been so proud of herself just a short while before, because she'd fought a man who would normally intimidate her and in the end had made him run. She knew Paco hadn't understood her elation. How could he? He never doubted himself. He wouldn't figure she'd see it as an accomplishment.

For Emilia, mere survival was an accomplishment, and no matter that she did it in a manner Taffy thought awful, she empathized.

As she checked the floor of the closet, her thoughts wandered back to the attempted abduction. "You know, Paco, when that thug was dragging me out of the club, he said something kind of strange."

"What?"

"That Ace Vigil wanted to *talk* to me."

Finished with the closet, Taffy wandered around the room, picking up and looking at books. The teenager who'd dropped out of school read everything from self-help to popular fiction—women's books with heroines who fought hard to rise against the odds, seeking a better life. Her eyelids began to sting. She didn't think she could stand it.

"I can imagine the kind of talking he meant. He knew you were going to be at Tropicale first chance you got, and he sent one of his goons after you."

"If he was after me physically, wouldn't he have come himself and tried to seduce me out of there?" Taffy reasoned. "He does think he's God's gift, you know. Maybe he did want to talk. Maybe he found out something about the man in the print. Or about Emilia."

"I just found out something about her," Paco said, digging in a drawer of the chest.

"What?"

"She didn't ditch this place voluntarily." From the drawer he pulled out what looked like a Bible. He lifted the cover. It was a hollowed-out container, and it was filled with money. "Her bankroll," Paco said thoughtfully. "If she were gone for good, she wouldn't have left this behind."

"Not unless she was too frightened to come back."

Paco set the fake Bible on top of the dresser and said, "Turn out the light."

"What?"

"Just do it."

Taffy flicked the wall switch, throwing the room into total darkness. She could hear Paco moving around. "What are you up to?"

"Checking something." He was at the window, opening the blinds, a dark silhouette against the poorly lighted city night. "If someone's out there, waiting for her, I don't see him."

The blinds shut with a snap, and Taffy turned the room light back on.

"Nothing makes sense anymore," she murmured.

She stared at the portrait of the Virgin Mary that sat crooked on the wall. Some instinct made her go closer to straighten it. Something interfered with the movement. A little force and it gave with a flapping sound. Curious, she removed the frame from its hook.

"What are you messing with that for?"

Taffy turned over the religious portrait to find what looked like a parking stub with an identifying number—it had been stuck into the side of the frame. She pulled it free, murmuring, "How odd."

Paco moved close enough to take the slip from her. "Trader Nick's," he read. "That's a pawnshop."

"So Emilia hocked something. Why hide the proof?" Taffy asked, replacing the portrait on the wall.

"Maybe she pawned something of value to someone other than herself," Paco suggested. "Something she doesn't want this other person to find."

A peculiar thrill of excitement charged Taffy. "And just maybe we'd better recover that something ourselves and see what secrets it holds."

"Trader Nick's is just down the block." Paco pulled out his wallet and inserted the stub. "I'll check it out in the morning."

"We'll check it out, right?"

"Yeah, yeah. *We* will check it out."

More satisfied than before, Taffy couldn't even work up a good annoyance. She was in too positive a mood. "By George, I think he's got it."

"So. Anything else you aim to accomplish tonight?" He checked his watch. "Sorry. This morning. It's already after one."

"I'm all out of productive ideas," Taffy admitted, though she was still seething with energy. Success was like sugar. Instant high. "Sleep *would* be the sensible thing."

Paco nodded in agreement. "Though I can't exactly bring you home to meet the folks. They're kind of old-fashioned that way."

"I didn't ask you to. I have a perfectly good bed in my own apartment. Surely you don't mind driving me. I don't want to leave my car on the street until I can get it fixed."

"It's not that I would mind driving you—it's just that you're not staying there."

Now she was getting annoyed. "Who says?"

"You've been attacked twice tonight," Paco reminded her. "Want to go a third round?"

Taffy swallowed. She hadn't been thinking straight. She'd rather face her apartment building in the cold light of day when plenty of people populated the street.

"All right. You have a point. No sense in tempting fate." Her luck was bound to run out sooner or later, and she voted for later. "I could check into a hotel."

"You are in a hotel and it's paid for. No one'll be looking for us here. Besides, if Emilia does show to collect her pawn ticket, we'll be waiting for her."

That made sense. She stared at the bed, which was full-size but looking smaller every moment. "I hope you're not a bed hog."

"What makes you think I might be?"

Her pulse threaded unevenly at the thought of sharing that small, intimate space with Paco. "Well, people who usually sleep alone—"

"Who said I usually sleep alone?" He lifted an eyebrow in challenge, but before she could get her wits together, he added, "I hope you're not suggesting I sleep on the floor tonight. After coming to your rescue in that alley, I'll be stiff in the morning as it is."

"I was only teasing." And trying not to choke of embarrassment. "Uh, if you're getting stiff, maybe you should take a hot shower."

"That's an idea." Turning toward the bathroom, he removed his watch, set it on the dresser, and in a low voice added, "Though a cold shower might be more effective at the moment."

Taffy couldn't miss his meaning.

While the water was running, she made every attempt to think of anything but Paco naked with thousands of droplets of running water caressing his body.

She hung up their jackets. Turned down the bed. Carefully set the stuffed animals on the chair.

Handling Emilia's personal items, she felt a sense of connection with the missing girl she could neither define nor explain. A connection that made her feel close to a stranger. And disturbed her.

She snapped on a night-light, turned off the overhead and waited for Paco to emerge from the bathroom. When he did a few minutes later, he was barefoot and his shirt was open, revealing the smooth, wet skin of his chest.

Taffy hurried past him, her gaze aimed at the floor.

"Don't worry," he called after her, laughter in his tone. "All's clear in there."

About to ask him what he meant, she noted the Roach Motel under the sink. Remembering the mess on the counter downstairs, she vowed not to get barefoot until she hit the bed. The dress would have to go, though, or she might ruin it. She hung it up on the back of the door, then put the black lace top back on and buttoned it. That and her footless lace tights would make pretty okay pajamas.

Taffy tried not to think of how provocative Paco might find them, and concentrated on scrubbing her face free of all that makeup.

Leaving the bathroom was one of the hardest things she'd ever had to do. To her relief and chagrin, Paco was already asleep. By the dim glow of the night-light, she could see him in bed, covered to the waist, chest bare, one arm thrown overhead so his muscles were displayed in all their glory. His chest rose and fell in a rhythm as deep as his steady breathing. Face toward her, his thick dark lashes brushed his cheeks.

She'd never seen a more beautiful sight.

Taffy sighed and wedged a hip on her side of the bed. She slipped out of her heels and slid under the covers, noticing that his trousers were on the chair with the stuffed animals. That made her speculate about exactly what he might or might not have on under the covers.

She tried to relax enough to go to sleep, she really did, but she was a bundle of nerves. No matter how hard she tried to convince herself that the dangerous excitement of the day kept her awake, she knew it was the seductive danger of being so close to Paco.

She twisted. Turned. Fidgeted. Counted sailboats. Tried to identify every pair of earrings in her extensive wardrobe. Nothing settled her down.

"You're getting more worked up by the minute." Paco's voice was low and amused and made her freeze in horror. "If you want, I'll sleep on the floor."

In a small voice, Taffy assured him, "That's not what I want."

"Then tell me."

A provocative invitation, and Taffy couldn't utter a single word if her life depended on it. She felt as if she were smothered by his nearness.

The mattress shifted as Paco turned and propped himself on his side. He reached over and took a curl from her shoulder and ran the long strands through his fingers. Though she knew it was impossible, Taffy imagined she felt the caress along her scalp and down the back of her neck and spreading to other sensitive and more intimate areas.

"You've got beautiful hair, especially when you wear it down like this. But then everything about you is beautiful. Your eyes." Paco leaned over and gave her a kiss as light as a butterfly at the corner of her right eye. "Your nose." His tongue wet the tip. "Your lips." His mouth brushed hers. "Your breasts."

Taffy giggled, then wanted to sink right through the mattress.

"What's so funny?"

"I'm covered in lace, and since you're a man you probably wouldn't know that makes your skin pretty sensitive already," she babbled. "I don't think I could stand it." When he started to withdraw, she quickly said, "But I wouldn't mind finding out for sure."

Paco lowered his head slowly, agonizingly, until Taffy couldn't bear his not touching her there. But when he got to her breast and rather than kissing it took the nipple between his teeth, she released a very feminine, very satisfied moan.

Paco released her and gravely said, "We don't have to do this."

"I think we do."

He found her mouth then, and explored it deeply. This wasn't like the other kisses they'd shared. This was earthy. Raw. Sexier than Taffy imagined a kiss could be. He wasn't touching her anywhere but on her lips. She was an ember ready to be ignited, her whole body longing to be singed by the experience.

He began stroking her. Teasing her through the lace until she tossed and turned, gasping for air. She wanted more. The feel of skin on skin.

"Whew! This is one hot outfit," she complained softly.

"I'm glad I'm not the only one burning up. Let's see what we can do about it."

He pulled her leggings down to her hips an inch at a time, mouth exploring and tasting as he exposed more skin. He took so long and worked so diligently she suspected she might explode.

When he entered her, she flamed from the inside out, the internal heat creating a slick of moisture between their bodies, a natural oil that lubricated their movements. Even so, her skin felt tight and prickly and pressurized beyond belief. The tension grew as Paco slowly, ever so slowly, moved within her, whispering her name like a litany.

A shaky breath coursed through her as he sank deeper inside. His neck pressed close to her mouth. She ran her tongue along the salty skin and felt a shudder ripple through Paco and into her.

Wrapping her legs around his back, she pulled him in tighter, unable to get enough of his heat. She was burning.... She'd never experienced anything like it.

Paco's lovemaking was the most glorious torch job of all.

Chapter Thirteen

Trader Nick's didn't open until noon. Paco stared at the sign and cursed their luck.

"Sounds like you got up on the wrong side of bed," Taffy said.

"Looks like we shouldn't have gotten out of bed at all."

"You know, some people use those things to sleep in," she informed him.

"Poor, misguided fools."

They'd spent nearly as much time making love as they had sleeping, and Paco didn't consider one waking moment they'd spent together as wasted. They made a good team, in and out of bed, no matter his previous opinion of their different backgrounds. Taffy obviously felt the same way. He only hoped her feelings went as deep as his. Happy despite their uncertain circumstances, he hugged her to his side and turned away from the pawnbroker's shop.

"What do you say we drop by my family's place until noon?"

"You want me to meet your mother looking like this?" Taffy sounded appalled.

"You look good enough to eat."

"That's what I'm afraid of."

Paco gave her an intimate wink that made her blush. "Mama probably won't even be there. And we've got a few other things to take care of besides cashing in the pawn ticket . . . like doing something about your car."

"Oh, all right," she acquiesced, grumbling, "but I'm keeping my coat on the whole time."

She needn't have worried about his mother, for he'd been correct. Only Marita was home. Taffy used the phone in the kitchen to contact her insurance company while Paco talked to his sister in the living room.

"What happened to her car?" Marita asked.

"A gang member used a brick to break the window and—"

"How do you know it was a gang member?" she snapped.

"Taffy was inside the car when it happened," Paco told her. "She saw them." Let her think about the scum she'd hooked up with. "Worse, they tried to overturn the car. To hurt her bad."

Marita turned pale and stared down at her shoes. "Mama and Papa went to the hospital real early this morning. Ramon woke up again."

Paco took a deep breath. "Thank God." Though the doctor had assured him his brother was going to be all right the day before, a tiny part of him had taken a wait-and-see attitude. "Was he awake long enough to talk?"

"Only to the doctor for a few minutes. Then he fell back asleep. Mama stayed with him while Papa opened the grocery. I said I would take over the store for a while this afternoon so he could go back to the hospital."

"Good."

Confused emotions played over Marita's beautiful face as she finally met his gaze directly. "Paco, I've been thinking. I'm sorry about what I said to you the other day. About your not belonging here."

"You were angry."

"And unfair. Why shouldn't you want the best life you can have? That doesn't mean you're not my brother anymore."

Paco saw Marita's admission as the one good result of Ramon's near tragedy. Too bad it had to take a horrible event to bring them closer together.

"I want a better life for all of us. Tito and Mama are set in their ways. They're never going to walk away from their lives here. But you and Ramon can, and I want to help you both do that. I love you."

"I love you, too." Tears in her eyes, Marita stood on tiptoe and hugged him.

Hugging her back, Paco remembered Taffy urging him to get closer to his siblings, not merely to offer to pay for their education. "I was thinking that maybe when Ramon gets out of the hospital we could spend a whole day together, just the three of us, just like we used to do."

"You mean you'll take us to the park and then to the movies, and we'll sneak in those big candy bars and then get yelled at by Mama when we can't eat dinner?"

They laughed together for the first time in far too long.

"We can do anything you want," Paco said.

He thought about bringing up Marita's relationship with Ace Vigil but figured that would be pushing things. One step at a time, he told himself. First Marita had to want to hear his opinion. Taffy had convinced him of that.

As if thinking about her made her appear, Taffy was there in the dining room doorway. True to her word, she was still wearing her coat. "I'm supposed to drive the car into Eddie's Auto Body and Glass Shop. If I get it in today, it'll be ready Monday afternoon."

"Then we'd better get a move on." Kissing his sister's cheek, he said, "See you later. If Ramon wakes up when I'm not there, you tell him I love him, huh?"

Marita nodded.

Taffy drove the damaged MG, Paco followed in the Jeep. It was noon by the time the paperwork was filled out and they were on their way back to Trader Nick's. Taffy sat as close as her seat belt allowed, her hand on his thigh distracting him.

"I'm glad you and Marita made up."

"So am I."

"Family's important. Technically speaking I have one, though I don't know what it's like to feel as close to them as you two seemed just now."

Paco remembered her saying her family always expected the worst of her. "You were *never* close?"

"Maybe a long time ago when I was a child, but even then, I was too undisciplined for my parents. Bitsy—that's my sister—did everything they expected of her. I guess, in the end, I did, too, only ironically it wasn't what they *wanted* of me."

Strange sort of logic, but Paco got the drift. "Sounds like I'm not the only one who has some major fence-mending to do. I thought you were going to call them."

"I did call them, and it made me feel better, but I'm not sure our fences can be mended unless I settle down with a man they approve of and spend my days having grandchildren and doing charity work. Proper work for a proper lady."

Paco didn't like the sound of that. The Darlings of this world would never approve of a man like him. Once he wouldn't have cared. But that was before he met Taffy.

One step at a time, he told himself, just like with his siblings. He would put this particular problem to the back burner for the moment.

"At least I have a start with Marita," he said with satisfaction. "Now all I have to do is find a way to convince her Ace is bad business."

"You didn't tell her about last night?"

"Only that gang members messed with your car and your life. The rest . . . no. She would have denied everything, especially the part about Ace having you abducted. I didn't want to get her defenses up. When this is over and it's clear to everyone who the bad guys are, her eyes will have to open." He only hoped that would be soon, before something could happen to Marita, too. "If only Ramon could tell us what went on the other night."

"Assuming he knows."

Paco recognized Ramon had been hurt worse than Taffy, and she still hadn't regained all of her memory. Furthermore, Ramon might have been caught by surprise.

He didn't have time to dwell on the subject, for they had arrived at the pawnshop. Trader Nick himself was a large greasy-looking man who seemed more interested in Taffy than in collecting his money.

"You ain't never been in here," he said, ogling her through the cagelike wall separating them. "I'd a remembered you if I'd seen you before."

"As would I," Taffy said politely.

He swirled a toothpick in his mouth. "You from the neighborhood?"

Paco quickly lost his patience. "Can we do business here, or what?"

"Hey, I'm a congenial kinda guy. I like making small talk with the customers."

"We're in a hurry."

"So I'll get your stuff already."

Taking the pawn ticket, Trader Nick shuffled into the back room and took his time. Taffy kept a calming hand on Paco's arm until the owner returned to the counter carrying a black leather briefcase. He took his money from Paco and shoved the case at him through the opening in the cage, but his attention stuck on Taffy.

"You come back now, little lady, you hear?"

"I hear."

Paco wasted no time in rushing her out the front door. Once in the Jeep, he opened the case, which at first appeared to be empty. Then he checked the back fold and found a pocket-sized matching leather notebook.

"Here's something." Paco began paging through the small book, Taffy hanging over his shoulder to see. Every entry was printed neatly if cryptically. "Hmm.

Some kind of personal reminders," he murmured. "And they've got to do with ward business."

"You mean this belongs to someone from Luce's office?"

"Right." He stopped at a page of addresses. "Look. These are all local." He scanned them quickly, tapping one in particular. "This one's right on the next block."

"What are you waiting for?" Taffy asked. "Get this buggy going and let's see exactly what we have here."

A moment later they were parked in front of a shell of an apartment building.

"Destroyed by a fire." Paco didn't know why he was so surprised.

"I thought the address sounded familiar," Taffy said excitedly. "This is one of the four addresses I gave to Eden to check out." Since she now had the book, she scanned the list. "Paco, here's another one of those buildings that burned. And a third! Somehow, the police missed the connection."

"What exactly *is* the connection, other than their being on this list?"

"Why don't we ride around and see if we can figure it out?"

While Paco drove, she went over the list again. "Odd. Three of the addresses from the newspaper clipping are on this list, but not the fourth."

"Maybe Emilia got hold of the notebook before the fourth fire."

"From who? One of her customers?" Taffy mused.

Within the hour, they'd gotten a look at every building on the list. A few had vacated apartments with plywood-covered windows, two others were totally abandoned.

When they got to the second, Taffy whispered, "Oh, my God. This is the one...the building where I hid from the arsonist."

And it, like all the others, was spray-painted with gang insignias.

"Here we are," Paco said, "back to the gangs."

"The newspaper article I read indicated gang involvement in the fires, I guess because it's obvious they hang around these buildings."

"And Ace tried to play innocent." Paco prayed Marita would wise up fast. He turned the Jeep and headed east toward Lake Shore Drive. "Since there's nothing more we can do here, I'll take you home."

Taffy was silent and thoughtful until they reached the lakeside expressway. "Paco, Ace is the one who said to look into the heart of the fires, remember? Why would he tell us that if he and his boys were the ones responsible for setting them? Maybe someone *is* trying to make the Latin Lovers look worse than they already are...to let them take the blame as part of some kind of cover-up."

Paco had to admit she made sense in light of the notebook. "What if it wasn't actually the Latin Lovers that someone was trying to hurt?" A possibility he hadn't before considered.

"Like who?"

"Someone might be trying to make Luce look bad. Incompetent—you know, unable to do the job she was elected to do. Maybe one of the rival gangs in the neighborhood..."

"Or one of Luce's *personal* rivals," Taffy added. "Someone who might want to make her look incompetent in dealing with the gangs she vowed to destroy."

Startled, Paco immediately asked, "Who? Gilbert?"

"What would he have to gain? It was David who wanted the job Luce got."

"You think her brother's punishing her for winning the election? That's not the way David operates. He's a social worker. He's devoted his life to helping others. No, Taffy, I've known David Sandoval all my life." Even as he made his denials, Paco remembered their conversation about Luce and had a sick feeling deep inside. "He used to be my best friend—"

"And Ramon is your brother," Taffy pointed out. "You were ready to blame him."

"I'd suspect Gilbert first. He's been acting suspicious."

"Gilbert could have been trying to protect Luce and his job, and he could have convinced Helen to help him."

Paco had to admit she might have stumbled onto something. "Man, that would be a damn shame if someone succeeded in ruining Luce's career."

"It's a damn shame when anyone's career is ruined," Taffy muttered. "Even a budding one."

"But you can't possibly know how hard she worked to get where she is." Paco was charged because, though he wasn't interested in Luce personally, he identified with her struggle. "How absolutely focused she's been all her life. This could destroy her, not just politically, but personally." He took a deep breath. "Her own brother? God, I hope it's not David. We'll definitely have to attend the benefit tonight. Maybe we can rattle some chains."

"Right. To the rescue," Taffy said, turning to stare out the window.

Paco had the feeling Taffy was upset, but he was too distracted to figure out why. That David could be an arsonist and a would-be murderer horrified him.

"Taffy, have you remembered any more about the man who attacked you?"

"Not really."

"Could it have been David?"

She hesitated for a moment, before saying, "He has the right build and coloring, but he seems so mild-mannered—nervous, even. I don't know. I honestly don't."

They were both silent and thoughtful for the rest of the drive. When they arrived at her place, Paco insisted on seeing Taffy up to her apartment.

"You don't have to. I know you want to get to the hospital."

"I also want to make sure you're safe." It suddenly occurred to Paco that Phantom and Peaches were in her place. "And I'd better collect my cats."

"You want to take them?"

She sounded both disappointed and resigned. Paco instantly recognized he needed to tread carefully here.

As they got in the elevator, he said, "I don't want to put you out. I don't even know if you like cats."

"They're not putting me out, for heaven's sake, and of course I like them. They don't eat all that much and they don't take up a lot of space." She was talking fast. As if she were nervous. "I wouldn't mind keeping them until you know where you're going to be staying in the future. It would be criminal to keep uprooting them when it isn't necessary.''

And Paco knew his response meant more to her than concern over the cats. ''Well, if you really wouldn't mind.''

''I really wouldn't.''

''Then they can stay as long as their master is welcome.''

She stared at him, wide-eyed. ''He's welcome anytime.''

''I'll remember that.''

Paco kissed Taffy and she relaxed against him. He could practically feel the stress flowing out of her. Good Lord, what in the world had been making her so uptight?

By the time she opened her apartment door, she was herself, to Paco's relief. And Phantom was waiting for them. One swipe of his legs and the cat ran to the kitchen area where she circled her food bowl and meowed indignantly. Taffy and Paco both laughed.

While Taffy opened the can of food, Paco whistled until Peaches came out of hiding. And when the food was divided into two bowls, Phantom ate while the shy cat was more interested in Paco's attention.

''It's nice to be loved,'' Paco commented as Peaches purred softly against his chest.

''Yes, isn't it?''

Taffy leaned back against the counter, a soft expression in her eyes. Approval? Affection? Or something more substantial? Paco certainly hoped so, and yet he hesitated putting his feelings into words. They were so new to each other and he had no idea what

Taffy wanted out of a relationship with him. He recognized he was growing on her, but last night might have been a fluke, a moment of comfort in a tense situation.

Well, more than a moment. More like half the night. The memory stirred him.

But when this was over and their worlds righted again, she might be more interested in fence-mending with her family than in continuing her relationship with him. The thought of her married to some society doctor or lawyer made him nuts, but he would never tell her so. He'd known she outclassed him from day one. When the time came, if letting her go would make her happy, he would do it and keep his regrets to himself.

Trying not to let the reality of their situation get to him any sooner than necessary, he gave each of the cats one last pat and ruffle.

"It's getting late," he said. "If I don't leave now, I won't be able to spend any time at the hospital before I have to go find a tux. Here's hoping I can rent one at the last minute."

"You could always be a rebel and not wear one," Taffy said.

"We'll see." At the door he pressed Taffy. "Promise me you won't leave this place, that you'll wait for me to come get you."

"Promise."

"And that you won't even open your door to anyone but me."

She merely lifted her brows, and Paco decided not to push it.

"Cocktails are at seven, so I'll pick you up at six-thirty or so."

"I'll be waiting breathlessly."

He ignored her sarcasm and gave her a quick kiss. Anything more and he didn't know if he could leave at all. Getting distracted now would be a real mistake.

He needed all his energies to flush out an arsonist.

TAFFY SIGHED and locked the door behind Paco. Normally she would revolt against someone giving her orders, but in this case, it was the wise thing to do. Besides, he'd only issued orders because he cared.

And she'd follow them this one time because she was in love.

A scary prospect.

Taffy couldn't help but think about the conversation they'd had on the way here. He'd been perfectly clear about how much he admired Luce for her determination and drive. He could relate to one of his own but not to her, Taffy realized.

Paco hadn't even thought about how her losing her position at Superior Promenade might make her feel. Then, again, she'd never exactly explained how important that job had been, financially or psychologically. Or that it had been her first opportunity to make something of herself.

So she was in love. What was she going to do about it? While neither social nor economic differences would stand in her way of getting her man, Paco himself was the problem. He'd done so much with his life. What would he want with a woman who'd wasted hers?

The phone jarred her out of the reverie. She picked it up on the third ring, before the recorder switched on.

"Hello."

"Taffy, darling, it's Eden."

"You got my message, didn't you?"

"Right, but it was too late to stop the wheels of progress. You may not be interested, but I thought I would call you about it just in case."

After finding the link in the notebook, Taffy wasn't about to turn down any information. "So what did your friend find out?"

"All four buildings were owned by different companies and had different officers and agents, so on the surface there's no connection. But, my friend went further and checked out the individual names. And guess what?"

"They're all related somehow?"

"Those companies and people don't exist. Fakes. Every one of them."

"What? How can that be?"

"I asked my friend the same question. It seems that companies have to register with the state, but the state doesn't have the resources to do regular background checks. It accepts the information as given."

"So the same people could actually have owned all four companies." Taffy was stunned. And elated. "Eden, maybe you'd better let me write this down."

She recorded the names of the phony companies followed by the fake officers and agents. Edgetown Investors, Lucky Properties, Broadway Realty and Rightway Management didn't mean anything to her, but maybe to Paco...

She thanked Eden and signed off, sending her love to Chick.

Brain spinning with the new information, she went upstairs to shower and wash her hair. Then she had to figure out what she was going to wear to what might very well be the social event of her life.

Basic black. And very, very sexy, due to the beading around the breasts and along the low-cut back. Finding the matching purse, she threw in the slip of paper with the company names so she wouldn't forget to bring it. The cats kept her company while she got ready, and even with the distraction they presented, she had time to spare. She went downstairs to wait, but she couldn't sit still. She put *Fire Goddess* back on her wall and stared at the artwork as if the goddess could share secrets.

"Do you know who torched Paco's building?" she asked, staring at the flames in the goddess's eyes.

The flames made her think of the article about Superior Promenade burning . . . the information about the fires in Luce's ward. Getting the newspaper, she turned to the inside page, and once more found the sidebar with the picture of the unidentified young woman who had died of smoke inhalation.

And she froze.

Her heart thudded in her chest and her mouth went dry.

She hadn't made the connection, hadn't realized . . .

But now she knew. Hadn't she looked at this face again and again over the past few days? She knew it almost as well as she knew her own.

Emilia Pino.

Emilia Pino was dead, had died in the case the investigators had related to the gallery fire.

Something akin to grief nearly overwhelmed Taffy. For a few moments the night before, she'd felt so close to the young woman who lived a sordid life but had big dreams. Taffy felt as horrible as if a friend had just died.

It all started making sense. A terrible perverted kind of sense. The notebook contained the addresses of the buildings that had been torched; Emilia not only had the notebook, but had hidden it at the pawnshop. If the notebook could lead the authorities to the guilty person, he would be desperate to get it back. And if he couldn't get it...

Emilia must have been murdered so she couldn't talk.

And *that's* why Superior Promenade had been torched, why Paco's place had been searched, then burned. To get rid of evidence that could convict someone of murder. To erase the connection between the dead girl and the man in the photograph!

The gang member was not only an arsonist, he was a murderer!

For days something about her attacker had been haunting Taffy, something she knew she'd missed. For days she'd avoided going back to that night and facing her terror. She was drawn back to the new-age canvas, to the *Fire Goddess* and the flames radiating around her. She stared at the vessel of burning oil in the goddess's hands... at the flames reflected in her eyes.

And inside her own mind, Taffy seemed to see fire exploding. Her heart pounded madly and she started to withdraw from the memory. But she knew it was time. She shut her eyes and allowed herself to remember that fateful night.

Smoke threatening to choke her, she was running down the stairs, seeking escape, the metal railing too hot to touch. She entered the inferno...a living, breathing entity. The roar around her was low and pulsating, and flames were shooting out at her, trying to devour her.

The belly of the beast.

She was running, running toward its mouth and safety. Footsteps slapped along the tile behind her. A shadowy figure. Threatening. She was running, trying to escape. The pain exploded along the back of her neck.

She was helpless. He was looming over her. And she saw him. Not his features. The sweatband. What else...something wrong with the picture.

Suddenly she knew. The thing that had been bothering her crystallized into one telling image.

The phone rang and the image shattered into a thousand tiny pieces. Her eyes opened and flicked to her clock. Six-thirty. Paco was right on time.

Chapter Fourteen

"Emilia Pino dead," Paco said hollowly as he stared at the lifeless woman whose image would haunt him forever. He set down the newspaper. "And we never even guessed."

"I should have known." Taffy sounded as if she felt downright guilty. "Why didn't I make the connection between the two photographs of her before?"

"Don't blame yourself. None of us is infallible, and with so much going on..."

Paco thought about all that Taffy herself had been through in the past several days. A less gutsy person might be a complete basket case, but she had bounced back from every incident.

"Besides, knowing she was dead earlier wouldn't have helped our investigation," he said logically. "If anything, it would have slowed us down. We wouldn't have the connection with the notebook because we wouldn't have gone looking for Emilia in the first place."

"I suppose you're right," Taffy conceded. "The notebook is important. There's something else I discovered, Paco, when I forced myself to concentrate on the gallery fire.''

"You remember what the arsonist looks like?''

"Mmm, his face was distorted by the shadows and flame. What I do know is that he wasn't a Latin Lover.''

"How?''

"No earring. The crucifix,'' she said, indicating her right ear. "He wasn't wearing it. And neither were those creeps who tried to turn my car over. I knew I was missing something!''

"The photograph I took of Emilia...'' Paco pulled a print out of his tux jacket. They looked at it closely. "That's his right ear. No earrings.''

"So Ace and Ramon were telling the truth.''

"Too bad Ramon didn't see who attacked him.'' Paco felt guilty that he'd suspected his own brother of torching his place when Ramon had actually come to see him to offer his help. At least he was conscious and protected. "Someone *has* been setting up the gang to take the blame for the fires.''

"Someone in the ward office.''

"David,'' Paco said. He'd hoped they'd been wrong about his old friend as he had about Ramon. "Who else could it be?''

"What about Gilbert?'' Taffy asked. "He could be the one.''

"Gilbert?'' Paco could imagine the press assistant being involved, he just couldn't imagine why. "You think he'd want to destroy Luce's career and put himself out of a job? That doesn't make any sense.''

"Nothing about this whole mess does make sense.''

"If only we could figure out a motive.''

"I almost forgot." Digging into her purse, Taffy told Paco about Eden's call. She handed him a sheet of paper with a list of companies and people. "I don't know if any of the names here will ring any bells, but I thought you should check them out."

Paco's gaze flicked over the list and was drawn back to one of the company names. A growing suspicion crept through him. And cold anger. If he was right, others would be angry, too. Maybe he could use that now to their advantage. Maybe it was time to call in reinforcements.

"Get your coat," he told Taffy.

He regretted she would be obscuring the vision that had entranced him the moment he'd walked in the door. Long jet-and-diamond earrings—for he was certain they were the real thing—sparkled through strands of her straight shiny blond hair, which was in perfect symmetry with the clinging beaded black dress. She would be the most beautiful woman at the benefit.

But once he helped her slip into the floor-length black fake fur, his mind turned back to the business of the evening. He was already formulating a plan of action, one that would have plenty of witnesses.

"C'mon," he said, rushing her out the door. "We have a couple of stops to make before we go smoke out a deadly arsonist."

THE WOMEN AND CHILDREN'S Protective League Dance was being held at The Water's Edge, a venerable old-money apartment building overlooking the lake at the very end of Luce's ward. Taffy had been there only once years before to visit with a friend of her mother's. Not much had changed, though. The first floor was still taken up with expensive boutiques and a luxurious paneled lobby with a wood-and-brass security desk.

The ballroom itself took up more than half the second floor. Cherry-wood walls glowed warmly under the light of a trio of crystal chandeliers. A massive green marble fireplace was the focus of a seating area at one end of the room. Two other walls held dozens of windows with a view of Lake Michigan obscured only by the sheerest of lace curtains. And gracing the buffet tables were the most luxurious linens, the most exclusive silver patterns.

An orchestra was playing, champagne was flowing, and in one corner, Luce Sandoval held court. Taffy spotted her immediately. Wearing a shell pink gown that draped her lush body as if she'd been sewn into it, the alderwoman was by far the most stunning woman present. She was a vision, sparkling, at home in the wealthy setting despite her impoverished background.

Paco noticed, too. "Quite an outfit Luce has on. Must be pretty expensive."

"There are several exclusive shops in the city and North suburbs that rent designer outfits, furs and jewels by the evening," Taffy told him.

"I don't see David," Paco said softly. "But Gilbert is certainly making himself known."

Indeed, Luce's press assistant was the center of a small knot of people, but whether from the force of his personality or the unusualness of his dress—a paisley-print dinner jacket with matching bow tie and cummerbund—she wasn't certain. Paco's assistant

Helen Ward stood nearby, just out of the circle, watching her date soak up the attention. She looked anything but happy.

"I wish Helen would wise up to that maggot," Paco whispered.

Taffy guessed that either the young woman was blindly in love or trapped by some darker motive that kept her with Gilbert. "She might already be wise."

Paco didn't respond, and Taffy was certain he understood her meaning. Continuing to scan the room, she finally spotted Luce's brother.

"Over by the windows," she said, touching Paco's arm. "There's David."

"I wonder what he's doing off by himself."

Drinking alone, David Sandoval seemed withdrawn, as if he didn't want to be there at all. Facing the lake, his right side was turned slightly toward Taffy...like the pose of the man in Paco's print. Her heart started hammering and she tried to make the visual to intuitive connection, but Paco's grabbing her by the waist and swinging her onto the dance floor interrupted her concentration.

"Should we really be doing this?" she whispered, tense just thinking of the surprises the evening was bound to hold.

"Relax and wait for the show to begin."

Taffy only hoped "the show" worked.

She woodenly moved to the music in Paco's arms, the contact nothing like that of the night before. Their dancing was almost impersonal. Impossible to relax when she was aware that one of the people in this room was responsible for a young girl's murder, a number of fires and attempts on both her and

Ramon's lives. That person had a lot to account for. And hopefully soon.

Her gaze skipped from David, still hanging back in the shadows, to Gilbert and Helen, who now seemed to be arguing, to the woman who was acting for all the world like a queen bee surrounded by her drones.

Luce Sandoval.

Frowning, Taffy concentrated on that idea and so was startled when Paco brought her to an abrupt halt. The music had ended. Some couples were leaving the floor, others changing partners.

And Taffy's nerves were unraveling bit by bit.

When Paco made no move to circulate, she said, "I don't feel like dancing. I could use a glass of champagne."

His expression surprised, he said, "Some food wouldn't hurt with that."

Her stomach protested at the thought of forcing something into it. "You've got to be kidding. Please, I really need something to steady my nerves."

Shrugging, Paco left her standing alone to stalk a waiter carrying a tray of filled champagne flutes. A moment later, Taffy heard a familiar voice that made her cringe.

"Taffy Darling, how nice to see you," came the over-melodious tones. "It's been absolutely ages."

She turned to the woman who wore her jewels like the spoils of a war. Ears, neck, fingers and both wrists were loaded with diamonds and emeralds. "Hello, Mrs. Tyler, you're looking as good as always."

"We missed you last evening. Your mother arranged that dinner expressly for you."

"Mother should have checked with me first before making plans."

Mrs. Tyler was one of her mother's dearest friends...and the biggest gossip around. Taffy was certain the woman would report every detail of what went on tonight.

"Are you here alone?"

"No, as a matter of fact I have a very handsome escort." Champagne flutes in both hands, Paco was approaching them, and she had no choice but to introduce them, thereby submitting him to the socialite's close scrutiny. "Leda Tyler, this is Paco Jones. Paco, Leda Tyler."

Paco handed one of the glasses to Taffy and said, "Mrs. Tyler, may I offer you some champagne?"

Her mother's friend acknowledged him with no more than raised eyebrows and a tight smile before turning back to Taffy.

"You certainly look your best tonight. No one would guess your terrible circumstances." Before Taffy could protest, the woman said, "Now, don't be embarrassed. Your mother told me how you lost your trust fund."

"*I* didn't lose anything. The funds were mismanaged."

"Yes, well, whatever, the results are the same. I hear you're next to destitute and you insist on getting some silly little job that couldn't possibly do." Mrs. Tyler waved her beringed fingers as if saying, *so much for that idea.* "Your Mother and I always thought my Arthur would suit—"

Taffy interrupted before Mrs. Tyler could finish. "Excuse me, but we really have to say hello to someone." Grabbing Paco's arm, she steered him away from the woman before Mrs. Tyler had the chance to tell Taffy how very unsuitable Paco was. She didn't slow down until they were near the ballroom entrance. "Sorry about that."

"Why didn't you tell me?"

"What? That my mother has obnoxious friends?"

"No. How important your job with Superior Promenade was to you. I thought you were a spoiled socialite taking work away from someone who really needed it."

"I figured that one out right away."

"But you never corrected me."

She glared at him. "Why should I have? Everyone, no matter their financial circumstances, should have the opportunity to do something satisfying with their lives." On the defensive, she downed half the flute of bubbly in one gulp. "Besides, if you couldn't like me for who I was, why should I tell you any different?"

His "I like you all right" smoothed her ruffled feathers. And so did the warmth in his dark eyes. "You're full of surprises."

"So I've been told." She hiccupped and covered her mouth in reaction.

A commotion at the doors cut off any further discussion of her circumstances. Taffy turned to see the door guard trying to stop the event from being invaded.

"I'm sorry, but you can't come in here dressed like that," the agitated man said as he was buffeted to the side.

Dressed in black leather jackets, wearing red sweatbands and crucifix earrings, half a dozen Latin Lovers pushed their way through the door, then parted to let Ace Vigil take the lead.

"Such rude behavior!" the guard said. "That does it—I'm going to have to call security!"

"Call anyone you want," Ace said loudly. "We're here as guests of Luce Sandoval."

A murmur rippled through the crowd and spread to every corner of the room. The orchestra stopped playing mid-number and the ballroom hushed.

Clearly losing her cool, Luce rushed toward the intruders, demanding, "What's going on here?" She aimed a venomous look at Ace. "What do you think you're doing, ruining my evening like this?"

Following on her heels, Gilbert said, "Get out while the going is good."

Ace smiled a silky, evil smile. "Or what?"

"You're causing a scene," Luce said, now bringing herself under control.

Her voice was moderated. Pleasant, even. Taffy figured she was playing to the audience avidly watching the scenario. Quietly David came up behind his sister, staying just out of the spotlight. Luce looked from the leader to the members of the gang, her expression only slightly tinged with distaste.

"Your being here is completely inappropriate," she added.

"Why?" Ace asked. "Aren't your constituents good enough to mingle with your new friends?"

Gilbert stepped forward. "The lady asked you to leave nicely."

Ace gave his paisley print a once-over. Laughter backed his voice as he said, "And who's gonna make me, Gilberto? A pansy like you?"

David stepped forward, but not quickly enough to stop Gilbert from lunging at the gang leader. He barely had his hands on Ace's chest before they were knocked away. When Ace went after Gilbert, he didn't miss. He shoved the press agent back into several women who screamed and pulled away.

Momentum and another shove kept Gilbert going. He fell back against one of the buffet tables. A silver candelabra rocked on its base, but a waiter saved it from toppling over.

As Gilbert gathered his resources and balanced forward, Taffy grabbed Paco's arm.

She was seeing Gilbert from the right side. No longer slicked back, his dark hair fell over his brow in greasy strings. And his stance was aggressive. The dim light threw his face into shadows and candle flames flickered around him.

And as Gilbert measured Ace, he went from being a sleazy buffoon to a far more threatening entity. His hand slashed out and he grabbed a carving knife from the table, holding it as he would a weapon.

Taffy blinked and stared as Gilbert came closer.

She was projected back to the fire, to the belly of the beast. She heard the low, pulsating roar... felt the unbearable heat... fought to breathe.

The shadowy figure loomed over her. Threatening. She was helpless...

...but she finally saw his face.

"He's the one," she ground out to Paco. "Gilbert's the man who tried to kill me in the fire!"

She blinked and Gilbert transformed back to the slick press assistant with equal speed as David gripped his arm and whispered something too low for anyone else to hear. David also removed the knife from Gilbert's hand.

"Security will be up here in a minute, Gilbert," David told him, loud enough for everyone to hear. "Let them take care of these hoodlums."

"We'll need more than building security." Paco pulled his arm free from Taffy's grip and stepped forward. "We'll need the police."

Voices rose across the room in renewed speculation tinged with horror.

"No arrests." Luce was reasonable now. "Nothing happened here that can't be forgotten. Let's not allow uninvited guests to ruin an important evening for so worthy a charity."

"But we were invited," Ace said. "To meet an arsonist. To meet whoever's been laying blame on the Lovers. To meet Emilia Pino's murderer."

"That's you, Gilbert," Paco said, pulling out the print. "And it's you in this photograph with Emilia Pino. You torched the gallery and my building to obliterate the connection."

Gilbert didn't even look at the print. "You've gone over the edge, Paco."

"Have I? Then this isn't you?"

The press assistant gave the photo a cursory onceover. "Hell, no. You're trying to frame me! That could be anyone."

Taffy then stepped forward. "But I didn't see just anyone at Superior Promenade the night it burned. I saw *you.*"

Gilbert backed away toward the entrance, but the Latin Lovers closed ranks and offered him no escape.

"You're mistaken," Luce told Taffy, her expression shocked and disbelieving. "You must be. I've known Gilbert for years. I give you my word of honor he can be trusted."

"This whole thing is ridiculous," Gilbert said, slicking his hair back from his forehead. He looked directly at Taffy. "You're mistaken."

His chameleonlike change almost convinced her until Helen Ward stepped out of the crowd, her face a mask of pain and fright. She spoke directly to Paco.

"I suspected Gilbert was involved in things I'd rather not know about, but I ignored my doubts about him until the prints were stolen."

"What made you think he was involved?"

"We were together the night before. It wasn't until later on, during the shoot down by the lake, that I realized my office keys were missing off my key ring. And then the office was rifled with no signs of a break-in."

"So you figured Gilbert used your keys to get in."

Helen nodded. "That night, after Gilbert visited my apartment, the missing keys were back with the others. That's why I came into the office on my day off, to see if I could figure out what he'd been looking for."

The Latin Lovers closed in around Gilbert. Eyeing them nervously, he moved away, toward the center of the ballroom, people there parting as if they were afraid they might be caught in the midst of a fight.

Then Gilbert bolted for the emergency exit.

And Paco stepped in front of Ace to go after the press assistant himself.

Taffy followed close behind, her gaze on the man she loved. Her heart thundered. She knew firsthand what Gilbert was capable of.

Determined that the bastard wasn't going to get away, Paco picked up speed, caught hold of the paisley-print jacket and swung him around. Gilbert was ready for him, catching him backhanded in the side of the face with a closed fist. A burst of pain and an explosion of light loosened Paco's grip. Gilbert pulled free. Paco immediately struck out but met thin air, then was thrown off balance when the other man kicked him square in the kneecap.

Gilbert was on the move.

But Paco wouldn't let an arsonist and a murderer go free.

Ignoring the excruciating pain radiating down his leg, he lunged at the press assistant, making body-to-body contact. The two men wrestled for a moment, trading a few close punches before stepping back and circling each other, Gilbert in top, aggressive form, Paco trying not to limp.

Gilbert swung and Paco sidestepped awkwardly. He grabbed his antagonist's wrist and with a jerk, threw him off balance. The press assistant went flying toward one of the buffet tables near the windows where a diamond-studded woman in black stood. He reached out to grab her. Her eyes widening, she remained frozen to the spot and shrieked hysterically.

Figuring Gilbert planned to take the woman hostage, Paco jumped him again and wrapped an arm across his throat. The woman was near fainting, but an elderly man pulled her away from the skirmish.

Gilbert was twisting and turning, though to no avail. He'd finally met his match, Paco thought with satisfaction. He turned a still-struggling Gilbert to face the crowd. Close by were Taffy, Luce and David, Ace and the Latin Lovers. The rest of the guests huddled together in small groups, staying at a safe distance murmuring amongst themselves, not one of them volunteering to do a thing.

"You're not going anywhere, Gilbert," Paco told him, "except to jail."

"If I go, it won't be alone!" Gilbert croaked. "I was only following orders."

Realizing Ace and his boys stood in a semicircle in front of them and would not let him get away, Paco finally let go. "So you admit your guilt. Who gave you these orders?" he asked, though he was certain he already knew.

Gilbert was silent for a moment, as if he were calculating his answer. He stared first at David. Then he turned to Ace Vigil, whose expression narrowed dangerously. Finally Gilbert's accusing gaze settled on the woman at David's side.

"Alderwoman Luce Sandoval is responsible for all of the fires . . . and Emilia Pino's death."

As the crowd issued a collective gasp, Luce sputtered, "H-he's c-crazy!"

"You're going down with me, sweetcakes." Gilbert turned to Paco. "Emilia, she knew too much about Luce's plans. She stole my briefcase and a notebook with private information. Only she figured things out—the buildings that burned, plans for the future. Smart little cookie."

"So she was blackmailing you?" Taffy asked.

"Yeah, me and Luce. Said we were her ticket out. Said she wanted to quit working the streets and go to school so she could get a real job. I told Luce to pay her enough to get her out of town, but Luce wouldn't let Emilia go because she could blackmail us forever. She gave Emilia some drug that knocked her out instead. Then she ordered me to burn the building with the girl in it."

Eyes glittering with unshed tears, Luce turned to Paco. He could hardly hear her over the speculations of the crowd. "You know me better than that, Paco," she stammered.

After all the wanton destruction he'd witnessed, Paco wasn't moved. "We checked into the buildings that burned in the ward. You should've been more clever when you named the fake corporations. *Lucky* Properties? C'mon, Luce."

Lucky had been her nickname in high school because she'd always gotten what she wanted. Paco had known she'd been a manipulative teenager, but he thought she'd matured into a forthright, giving woman.

"Did you tell your flunky to kill me, too?" Taffy demanded.

"You just got in the way, doll," Gilbert said.

Making Paco yearn to take the man's throat between both hands and squeeze the breath out of him.

Luce was looking around wildly, her gaze finally settling on her brother. "David. It was David who gave me the damn nickname! He set me up!"

David Sandoval sadly shook his head and appeared stricken at her betrayal. "Don't, Luce. I can't protect you anymore. I tried to stop you, but you wouldn't listen to me. I never even suspected how far you meant to take this. I told you before, I won't go to jail for you."

"But you *know* I was only trying to get rid of the gangs. You agreed to help me. To rid the ward of scum like that!" she said, pointing to Ace Vigil.

"But not in the way you went about it," David said.

And Ace added, "If you're ordering the burning and killing, who's the scum?"

Paco couldn't believe what he was hearing. "Let me get this straight. You bought buildings and burned them to get rid of the gangs?"

"It was the only way," Luce stated. "Those buildings in the neighborhood were hotbeds for gang activity. They made them their clubhouses, stored stolen goods in them and pushed drugs out of them. You see, I had to get rid of those buildings so I could get rid of the gangs once and for all."

"And collect some nice insurance settlements," Paco reminded her.

"So I made a profit." Luce shrugged that away. "My motives were pure."

"Your motives stink, Luce."

"You have to understand," she said, her voice straining with a rising hysteria. A sob caught in her throat, and when she blinked, tears washed rivulets of mascara down her perfect cheeks. "Everything I did was for the good of my constituents. I was doing it for them," she told Paco, her arm sweeping the room to include everyone. "To get their approval."

"That your story, Gilbert?" Paco asked.

"Hey, she paid me good. What can I say?"

Luce was going on, as if she were desperate for people to believe her. "I always knew I could be somebody, and now I am. Look at me." She turned to Paco. "Am I anything like the girl you knew who grew up on welfare and food stamps?"

"You're exactly like her." Paco had been fooled as had the people in her ward who had voted for her... and yet, he had known all along there was something wrong, no doubt why he'd never taken the bait when she'd come on to him. "You just look more expensive."

Luce shrieked and tried to claw his face. David caught her wrist and quietly said, "My sister's not well. She needs professional help."

Ripping her arm free from his grasp, Luce moved out of his reach. "I was doing you all a favor!" she shouted, backing away from the people who were now staring at her in horror. "Why can't you see that?"

Backing away, she tripped and threw her arms out wildly. Her hip rocked the buffet table and one hand knocked into a candelabra that toppled, sending its three lighted candles shooting along the linen table-cloth. Fed by the melted wax, the flames flared and quickly spread along the table's length. Trying to get her balance, Luce pulled the cloth to the floor. The old wood caught immediately.

People began screaming, their voices loud enough to drown out Paco's "Don't panic!"

Before his horrified eyes, The Water's Edge ball-room became the wick to a flaming torch.

Chapter Fifteen

Mesmerized by the flames that burst into full-blown glory before her very eyes, Taffy froze while pandemonium broke out around her. She stood between the majority of people in the room and the exits. Within seconds, she was surrounded, buffeted, caught in the crowd hysteria. Some people were screaming and crying, others shouting to one another. All were jostling for position, desperate to get out with their lives.

"Taffy!"

She heard her name, turned in confusion. "Paco?"

"I'm over here!"

Now separated by half a ballroom, Paco waved to her with his free hand, the other hand keeping hold of Gilbert Koroneos. And to their credit, the Latin Lovers remained nearby as if ready to railroad the arsonist and murderer themselves. The press assistant paid none of them any mind, but watched the conflagration with something akin to ecstasy washing over his sleazy face.

Taffy forced herself to move, to try to make her way toward them. To Paco. But then she heard David, saw him being swept to the entrance by the panicked masses.

"Luce. Luce! What are you doing?"

Taffy whipped around and shoved through the crowd to see Luce running blindly away from her brother. Taffy had already switched directions before she even made up her conscious mind that she would follow Luce. After everything she'd been through, she wasn't about to let the woman responsible for so much destruction escape her just dues.

Around her, the fire was spreading fast, fueled by the oxygen coming through open windows. No longer confined to the floor, flames devoured the curtains and climbed the paneled walls. Ash floated through the thick air and insidious smoke wrapped its deadly tentacles around those trying to escape.

Her size a disadvantage, Taffy fought hard against the crowd. Her progress was slow, but ahead of her, she could see Luce was panicked and clumsy and even slower. The dark-haired woman was choking on the smoke, and her hands were at her throat. The pearls popped and with a screech, Luce dropped to the floor to retrieve them.

"Taffy, this way!"

Taffy threw a quick glance over her shoulder, saw Paco coming after her, arms flailing forward as if he were swimming to cut through the surging surf of bodies. She didn't slow, not even when the smoke blurred her vision, filled her throat, whirled her back to that night less than a week before.

The horror rushed in on her and she had to fight to keep herself from panicking.

Finally she broke through the perimeter of the crowd just as Luce got to her feet, both hands filled with what was left of her pearls. Covered with soot but looking no less magnificent than she had earlier, she was searching wildly for an escape.

"Luce!" Taffy shouted. "There's nowhere to run!"

Luce teetered, confusion etching her features. Then they turned menacing. "I had a purpose to my life!" she screamed at Taffy. "I made something of myself!"

"Something sick. But you're through with destroying and killing and hurting."

"It's *your* fault. If it weren't for you, no one would know. And who are you, anyway?" Luce taunted. "A worthless nothing. You're a rich man's daughter who always had everything she wanted!"

Even though Taffy knew that wasn't altogether true, the words stung. She grabbed Luce's arm and a handful of pearls went flying. With a strength born of anger and fear, she forced the larger woman several yards back toward the emergency exit before Luce ground them to a halt. Just as Taffy turned, Luce struck out, opening her fist so the last of the pearls went flying. Her palm smacked Taffy's cheek.

"Let go of me!" she screamed.

Taffy was hardly a match for Luce in her rage. The alderwoman pulled her arm free and shoved Taffy. But Taffy wasn't about to give up so easily. She went after Luce who was already moving. She snatched at her dress, which ripped across the hip.

"Now look what you've done!"

And if she hadn't recognized it before, Taffy saw the madness in Luce's eyes. A madness grown from a voracious hunger for status and power. Luce grabbed the front of Taffy's dress and pulled. Glass beads popped and sprayed while Taffy tried to catch on to Luce's arm again. Then Luce grabbed a fistful of blond hair and yanked. Before Taffy could react, she was on the floor with Luce on top of her. They rolled over the pearls, stopping when they hit a hot spot.

The floor below them was ready to ignite. And with Luce astride her, Taffy couldn't move, couldn't breathe.

Suddenly the weight was lifted from her chest and she realized Paco had reached her just in time. But as she rose with his help, she saw Luce behind him...picking up a fallen candelabra...swinging.

"Paco, look out!"

He turned too late. The heavy silver candlestick crashed into his forehead, and he buckled to his knees.

Flames slicked around them. Closer. Higher. Hotter. Inhaling smoke, Taffy started coughing and couldn't stop. Even so, she struggled to get a barely conscious Paco back up to his feet, while Luce separated herself both physically and mentally from the crisis.

"Everyone will remember me. I won't be a forgotten nobody!" Luce announced.

She walked directly toward the heart of the fire. Her expression became relaxed—peaceful, even. Her back straightened and her head lifted with a sense of unbelievable dignity as she opened her arms and embraced her destiny.

The shell pink of her dress torched in an instant, flaming straight up to her dark hair.

Stomach revolting, Taffy couldn't watch.

"C'mon, Paco," she said between coughs. "Help me. We've got to get out of here."

She turned her head into his chest and with arms around his waist, took the brunt of his weight as they stumbled toward salvation and fresh air. Stunned by what she'd just seen, she could hardly think as they joined the stragglers.

Ace Vigil was waiting for them.

And as the firemen were entering, hoses spraying, Ace hooked an arm around Paco's back from the other side and accepted his weight.

Together, Taffy and the gang leader walked Paco away from the raging inferno and certain death.

"YOU DID IT. You told me you would and you did," Paco said wanly from his seat on the back of the ambulance.

A paramedic was just finishing with the bandage that covered half his forehead. And beyond stood the fire engines and the smoking building, the blaze now under control.

"You returned the favor, just like you promised," Paco went on. "You saved my life. Now you don't have to worry about owing me anymore."

Taffy forced a smile to her lips. She should be happy. She was out of danger. They were all out of danger. And she was free of any further obligation. That's what Paco was telling her. She didn't owe him anymore.

"Let's get you inside," the paramedic was saying. "We're taking a little trip to the hospital where you'll get checked out more thoroughly."

"Nah, I'm fine."

"We can use restraints," the paramedic threatened.

"All right. As long as she can come with me."

"Maybe you can share a room with Ramon," Taffy joked tightly.

"Different hospital," Paco said, settling on the stretcher inside the ambulance. He didn't seem to notice how subdued she was. "Hey, aren't you coming?"

"You'll be all right," she said, backing away. "You don't need me."

He yelled, "Taffy," as she turned and practically ran to the corner where she checked for a bus stop.

A hand caught her upper arm. "You look like you could use a ride home."

She gave Ace Vigil a wary look, but his usual cockiness was put away for a moment. "You and how many other Lovers?"

"Just me."

Nodding, she followed him to his car. She could handle anything, she told herself. Anything but losing Paco. Luce's words still stung. Even though the woman had been misguided and mad, she had been right about Taffy. A worthless nothing.

She was quiet on the drive home. Ace did most of the talking.

"Never thought I'd hand someone over to the cops," he said. "But I was glad to give Gilbert to them. What a scary son of a bitch. Wouldn't take his eyes off the fire until he was forced into the cop car. Probably woulda liked to have joined the alderwoman in her moment of glory."

Taffy's stomach clenched at the memory. The vision of a human torch would be with her forever. Lots of things would.

They were nearing her apartment house when Ace said, ''That Jones, he's all right.''

''Thank you for helping me get him out of there.''

''Yeah, well thanks for clearing me and the boys of those fires.''

''We sound like a mutual admiration society.''

''A who? Oh, yeah. You're all right, too. Like I said before, that Jones is a lucky guy.'' When Taffy didn't respond, he added, ''Unless you're aiming to dump him.''

''I think you've got it from the wrong direction. He doesn't need me anymore. He said so.''

Ace double-parked in front of her entrance. ''That's not what I heard. I heard a guy who's nuts about you, thanking you for saving his life.''

''We hear what we want to.''

''Yeah, maybe we do. You oughta think about that before Jones comes looking for you.'' As Taffy got out of the car, he added, ''And if you're dumb enough to send him packing, you know where you can find me.''

Taffy wanted to play into Ace's fantasy of Paco being ''nuts'' about her, but she held back. She didn't want to get her expectations up only to have them dashed. Now that the crisis was over, she wouldn't be pestering Paco. He would have no reason to see her unless he really wanted to. He cared, at least on some level. She knew that. But she was wrong for him. And he would realize that when he took time to think things through. Then mere caring wouldn't be enough.

Entering her apartment, she was pleased to see both Phantom and Peaches waiting for her. No sooner had she said, "What loyal little kittens," than they sniffed the air, turned tail and ran.

Of course. She reeked with smoke from the fire. Bad memories for them, too.

Taffy wandered through the dimly lighted apartment, wondering how she was ever going to get to sleep. A hot shower would relax her and get her clean. Thinking about snuggling with Phantom and Peaches reminded her of Paco and their single night together.

If only she could curl up in his arms, she would be sure to sleep...

A knock at her door startled her. Had one of her neighbors seen her coming in looking bedraggled and was now checking on her? The last thing she wanted to do at the moment was give some lengthy explanation to a person she hardly knew.

The knock came again, this time more insistent. She might as well get it over with.

Crossing to the door, she rose on tiptoe and peered out the peephole. Paco—looking grungy, exhausted and very definitely ticked! Taffy's pulse jumped and she took a deep breath, then let him in.

"Why aren't you at the hospital?"

"What do you mean I don't need you?"

Both questions asked simultaneously.

"You first," Taffy demanded, hoping to regain her equilibrium while he explained.

"I *need you* more than a doctor."

"How do you know you don't have a concussion?"

"Don't get off the subject."

"I'm not," she insisted, walking to one of the windows where she stared out at another former warehouse. Her heart was pounding with hope...and fear of disappointment. "We're talking about why you didn't go to the hospital."

"Because I saw the woman I love walk away from me like she meant it." Behind her, Paco placed gentle hands on her shoulders. "No threats from a paramedic were going to keep me from going after her!"

"Love?" she echoed in a small voice. She turned to meet his serious gaze.

"You need a definition?"

"No, but you need your head examined." She eyed the bandage.

"If that was a joke, I'm not amused."

"No joke." She sighed. "Paco, we've been so caught up in this game of find-the-criminal—that made us depend on each other and turn to each other for comfort. But now it's finished. And so are we."

His serious expression turned angry. "You may be finished, but I'm not."

"That's adrenaline talking."

"It's my gut talking. I can't be without you, it's that simple."

"It's not that simple. You said it yourself. We're from different worlds."

"Who cares?"

"You do."

"Not anymore."

"Then I do."

Various emotions flickered over Paco's features, ending in resignation and disappointment. "So I'm not good enough for you, is that what you're saying?''

Taffy looked at him in amazement. "Just the reverse. I'm not good enough for you. Look at all you've done with your life. You started with nothing, but you've made something of yourself professionally, and you're trying to change people's attitudes through your personal photography. You're a success. How can you want to be with a woman who never did anything worthwhile?''

"You've got a big heart and more guts than any woman I've ever met. Finding a murderer isn't exactly nothing.''

"I didn't do that by myself.''

"I couldn't have done it without you. We did it together. A team. I can offer you a partnership. Love. Respect. What I can't offer you is the kind of life-style you're accustomed to. At least not yet.''

"Life-style? Are you kidding? I don't even know where next month's rent is coming from.''

"That's easy. I need a place to live and you obviously need a roommate. I can cover expenses while you look for a job. Better yet, you can work for me.''

Hope filling her despite all reason, Taffy shook her head. "I've already started my job search. I'm going to do this on my own. I won't take a handout because you feel sorry for me.''

"Sorry for you? I feel lots of things for you, lady, but sorry isn't one of them." Paco paused and said, "You didn't object to the roommate part.''

"Well . . . it would be a shame to move the cats just now when they're settling in.''

"So you'll agree to my proposal for them.''

"And to make their master happy," she said.

"Peaches, Phantom," he called. "Fresh tuna tomorrow."

"A reward? What about me? What do I get?"

"What do you think?"

No more guessing games. Before another word could cross her lips, Paco had them busy. His kiss torched a flame in her heart and soul that Taffy suspected would never be put out.

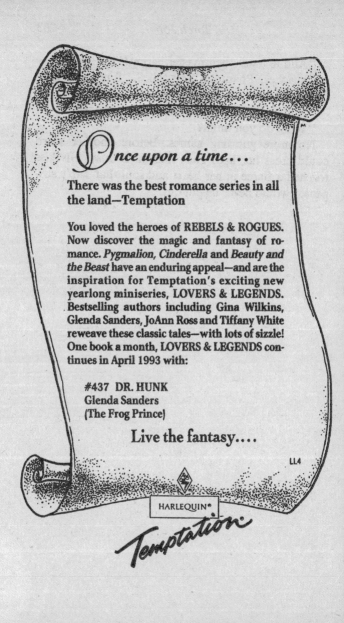

HARLEQUIN PRESENTS®

A Year DOWN UNDER

In 1993, Harlequin Presents celebrates the land down under. In April, let us take you to Queensland, Australia, in A DANGEROUS LOVER by Lindsay Armstrong, Harlequin Presents #1546.

Verity Wood usually manages her temperamental boss, Brad Morris, with a fair amount of success. At least she *had* until Brad decides to change the rules of their relationship. But Verity's a widow with a small child—the last thing she needs, or wants, is a dangerous lover!

Share the adventure—and the romance—
of A Year Down Under!

Available this month in
A YEAR DOWN UNDER

THE GOLDEN MASK
by Robyn Donald
Harlequin Presents #1537
Wherever Harlequin books are sold.   YDU-M